The Things Boys Do

Growing Up In A Small Town

The Things Boys Do

Growing Up In A Small Town

John C. Wall

iUniverse, Inc.
New York Bloomington

iUniverse books may be ordered through booksellers or by contacting:

iUniverse
1663 Liberty Drive
Bloomington, IN 47403
www.iuniverse.com
1-800-Authors (1-800-288-4677)

ISBN: 978-1-4401-3543-9 (sc)
ISBN: 978-1-4401-3544-6 (ebook)

Printed in the United States of America

iUniverse rev. date: 03/31/2009

Contents

Foreword

When I was very young I thought that, "Bigger was better." The biggest package under the Christmas tree was always my first choice. As I grew older, my theory was proven false. This was particularly true comparing growing up in a small town with that of a large city. For me, the small town of Hugo, Oklahoma, was ideal. I came along in 1933 when the country was experiencing a deep economic depression. The citizens of Hugo had pulled together to survive. They became a stronger, more loving, community minded, group of people. Everyone looked out for each other. There were few locked doors in town. I'm not sure we had a key to our house. It was a time of innocence in America. I grew up under the guidance and supervision of what has become known as the Greatest Generation. My friends and I were instilled with the morals, and work ethic of that day.

Plans for the city of Hugo were drawn in November, 1901. The number of people living in and around town varied through the years, but leveled out around seven thousand. That number remains the same today. The town's economy is based mainly on the railroad and agriculture industries. The area is a fisherman's and hunter's paradise. Many sportsmen travel to Hugo to take advantage of this situation each season. Of course this too, adds to the local economy. The people are hard working and friendly.

I stated earlier that when I was growing up everyone looked out for each other. This included keeping an eye on youth activities. I recall many adults, other than my parents, correcting me when I was out of line. Parents had a network that spanned the town like a blanket. If I got into mischief, I knew my mother would know about it by the time I arrived home. Their system was very effective, and it kept us on our toes.

I left Hugo in 1951 to serve in the military. After my tour of duty was completed, my professional career took me elsewhere, but my family and I have returned many times. During our visits stories from my childhood provide entertainment and amusement as we drive over familiar streets. My family knows the gist of my tales but insist that I tell them, one more time.

Class reunions I have attended are special to me. I'm always excited when I arrive, and anxious to see my former classmates. Friday evenings we have a great meal, listen to recordings from the forties and fifties and swap stories of our youth. The following day we tour the high school building. We speak of Ms. Lynn, our English teacher, and I recall her favorite comment to me, "Why can't you be more like your brother?" We look at our class rooms and metal lockers which line the hallway. We think of Ms. McBrayer, Mr. Fredrick, Ms. Glenn, Coach Parker, and others. Each person seems to trigger a special memory. There are other enjoyable activities throughout the weekend. Although I did not realize it at the time, these friends, teachers, facilities and many people of Hugo had been a great blessing to me.

What fun we had growing up! Sure, there were some things we didn't care to remember. But it reminded us we enjoyed the good times and survived the bad. It gets a person in the right frame of mind to face the future. I say: Enjoy every day and look for something good. When the most recent reunion was over, my trip back home was much more pleasant. I noticed the beautiful grass meadows, blue skies, and birds swooping back and forth. I was beginning to notice some of the abundant blessings that I had been missing. I approached the road under construction which I had encountered on my way to Hugo. This time instead of complaining about the condition, I was thankful that the remainder of the road was in fine shape. Earlier I had been like the guy who complained about not having a car in his garage, but overlooked the fact that he had a garage.

We live in a fast world. Did the teens in the fifties ever think that cars would travel over 200 hundred miles an hour or airplanes would travel at supersonic speeds? We get caught in the fast pace: not taking time to analyze or enjoy our every day blessings. I'm sure the writer of the song "Count Your Blessings" had experienced a speed trap and was warning others to slow down and take note. We spend much of our time looking forward, but sometimes it's nice looking back to different times. That's what these stories are about.

Through the urging from my family I have written this book. The stories and characters are fictional. It is my hope that the reader enjoys the stories as much as I have had telling them all these years.

CHAPTER 1

Chief Justice

Being the Chief of Police for Hugo was not a bad job. In a town of 7,000 there was not a great deal of serious crime. Most people knew each other, and it was difficult to do anything without everyone being aware of what you were up to. Bob Baker had been on the police force for four years before advancing to the position of Chief. Bob was born in Hugo and except the years spent at college and military duty, he had lived in Hugo all of his life. He was well-liked by the town's people and had a good reputation among the law enforcement community.

Bob was not always a by-the-book type of policeman. When a young person got into minor trouble, he would sometimes allow them leniency but not before they had given a good scare. After talking with the parents he would lock the youth in one of the empty city jail cells and leave them for several minutes. Upon his return he would ask, "How does it feel to be locked up without hope of escape? Well, if you don't stop acting like you did tonight, you are going to get a whole lot more of that feeling. Now get out of here, and I don't want to see your ugly face around here again. Ever!" It was agreed that the parents would not mention that they had been contacted. Bob knew this was a very effective lesson for most kids since he had received the same treatment when he was young. As the years passed, he was very grateful that someone cared enough to teach him what could result from his irresponsible actions. During his career in law enforcement he had seen the effect that five or ten minutes of unthinking acts could have on people's lives. If he could redirect someone's path in the right direction, he felt justified in relaxing the rules of law enforcement.

Bob's work day generally started with a trip by his office at City Hall to see if anything unusual had occurred during the night. Afterwards, he would drop in at Don's Café to have his morning cup of coffee. Also, he could measure the pulse of the city and catch up on the latest news being discussed by the customers.

Bob finished his coffee and returned to the office. There had been a report of domestic violence, and one of the deputies had responded. Bob's first thought was of Carol and Gil Walters. It would not be the first time they had been called to their house to calm Gil down when he had overindulged. Bob was very fond of Carol, and they had been friends since she was a little girl. He was relieved to hear that the report had not come from her address. He felt sorry for Carol, since she was married to what he privately referred to as a "scum sucking dog". No one knew exactly what that meant, but they were sure it was not meant as a compliment.

Carol's marriage to Gil Walters had not been pleasant. At first they were happy, but after several months of married life Gil's attitude began to change. He began to drink excessively and was particularly mean when he was drunk. Carol was young and a very attractive woman with an extremely fine figure. If Gil saw a stranger eyeing his wife, there was always trouble. In truth, most men in town enjoyed looking at her as long as their girlfriends, wife's, or Gil were not around. Carol had never encouraged anyone for their attention. Actually, she dressed in such a way as to hide her looks, but some things you just cannot cover entirely. The local men knew it was not in their best interest or Carol's to be too friendly with her. Aside from Chief Baker and Gil's brother Bill Walters, all of her close friends were women. Several times she had been seen with bruises on her arms. She would tell anyone who asked that she had run into a door or a cabinet. Most people pretended not to notice for fear of embarrassing her. Some very close friends had spoken to her about Gil's actions. Each time Carol would defend him saying, "Gil's abuse has not been extreme, and I'm certain that things will get better in time."

Gil was the younger brother of Bill Walters. They were as different as night and day. Bill was a fine, upstanding member of the community, and Gil was the town thug. He owned three beer joints near the river south of town. It was rumored that he sold more than hamburgers and beer, but he had never been charged with any illegal activity. His taverns were located outside the city limits and beyond Bob's jurisdiction. That was a matter for the sheriff. When Gil was involved in a business deal that required muscle, some of his employees would be called on to assist. They were known around town as Gil's Gang or "G-G" men. For the past three years Gil and his gang had been involved in every shady activity within fifty miles. He had bullied and terrorized several people in the area, but Gil was smart when he selected his victims. He would pick those who would not fight back because they were afraid or those that did not care to have the sheriff investigating their activities.

Bob's relationship with Gil was somewhat civil, mainly because he did not want to cause problems for Carol. Gil did not think much of the chief but was polite toward him for obvious reasons. Bob longed for the day when he could lock Gil up and throw the key away, but when the opportunity came, the ill used would either not press charges or not be willing to testify. Gil's violent actions and reputation was becoming more serious and widespread. Bob knew that one day he would go too far.

After completing his day's work, Bob instructed deputy Hank Green, and the three night shift personnel to "Keep a close watch on the Saturday night activities and to call him if anything unusual happened." Otherwise, he would see them in the morning before church. There were several night spots in town. The Cottonwood Club was the most popular, but if there was trouble, it generally originated from the Bee Hive Inn. Their motto was "Bring Your Honey and Buzz Around". Sometimes their buzzing got out of hand. That club would require the most attention. Bob took a final drive around town and went home to enjoy what he knew would be a fine supper with his wife, Jane, and their two children, Joe and David. After eating, the family generally would walk several blocks around the neighborhood to get some exercise. Sometimes they would be joined by friends along the way. This evening was no exception. Bob took his football and threw passes to the kids as they walked. It made for stop-and-go walking, but everyone enjoy it. He dreamed about his two boys becoming star players for Hugo High and possibly going to the college ranks. His dream was dimmed a little when his youngest expressed a desire to play in the band. Bob was, at first, repulsed by this idea, but later decided that it would be all right if that's what David really wanted. However, he would continue to throw him passes, just in case. Daylight was just about gone when they arrived back at the house. It was time for the kids to take their baths and lay out their clothes for Sunday church. Bob wanted to repair a cabinet door before going to bed. Jane had asked him to fix it several weeks ago, and he thought his excuses were just about exhausted. With the cabinet work completed and all was ready for Sunday, Bob turned off the lights commenting, "It's been a great day."

Sundays in Hugo are usually quiet with many of the citizens attending the church of their choice. Some of the remaining people would be doing chores or sleeping late after a big evening at one of the late-night entertainments. Bob attended the Baptist Church where he worked with the youth group. Coach Parker and several members of the football team also attended regularly. This Sunday before the worship services began the coach and players were asked to stand so they could be recognized for their fine play winning the district title. The general topic of the sermon was overcoming problems and being victorious in life, even when things seemed hopeless. The timing of that sermon topic and Friday's football game was not lost on the congregation. There were many comparisons made between life and a football game. Bob noticed the youth were listening to every word without the usual passing of notes, whispering, and restlessness.

The following day Bob had just finished supper when the phone rang. Before he could say hello, his deputy spoke,

"There's a wreck on the highway east of town.

"Do you know who's involved?" Bob asked.

"No. And we're not sure it's inside the city limits. The caller who reported the accident was uncertain of her location. Anyway, I have dispatched a unit along with an ambulance. Do you want to go?"

"Yes, I'll take a run out there and see if I can help. Have you notified the sheriff's office?" Bob asked.

"No. Not yet, but I'm going to do that now. I wanted you to know before I call him." the deputy replied.

"These things seem to happen every year when we have our first snow." Bob mumbled under his breath. "I don't know when the people around here are going to learn how to drive on snow." Approaching the location of the wreck, Bob was aware that he was outside the city limits. He would not have an official part in the investigation. He drove several yards beyond the place where a car had gone off the side of the highway. Bob knew other emergency vehicles would need room to maneuver. He would assist the ambulance crew or perform traffic control until the sheriff and his people arrived.

When Bob got out of his patrol car, he left the emergency light on to signal danger to any oncoming traffic. As he walked toward the location of the wreck, his flashlight highlighted some car tracks in the snow along the side of the road. The tracks indicated that two cars had been parked. The front car tracks appeared to have been blocking the other car. It had been parked at an angle that would have prevented the other car from moving forward. There were several foot prints in the immediate area. Bob didn't take time to look closely at the prints but did notice that the smaller prints had a triangle-shaped logo on the heel. Although what he had just seen was interesting, his thoughts quickly turned to the problem of the wreck.

Bob stopped at the spot where the vehicle had left the road. There was a deep drop off from the highway, and the car had traveled several feet downward before striking a large tree. The deputy and medical attendants had worked their way down to the wreck. Bob could see light coming from inside the car. He yelled down to find out if the driver was hurt and if there were other passengers in the car.

"Driver appears to be dead and there are no passengers. We're getting ready to come up. When I holler, take hold of the rope we left up there and pull." came the reply.

While Bob was waiting, he looked at the tracks the car made as it went over the embankment. There was no sign of skidding. There were foot prints with the same triangle logo on the heel that he had seen several yards up the road. A closer look revealed that the left foot print had a small grooved cut near the big toe area of the sole. A shout "Pull us up!!" came from below. Bob put his flashlight away, grabbed the rope, and began to pull. Two men from the Sheriff's Department arrived and joined in. By the time the rescue party had reached the road, the sheriff had arrived. Others arriving included a reporter from the local news paper and several teenagers who were looking for some excitement. A group gathered around the stretcher while the medical personnel did another exam before loading the body in the ambulance. The reporter asked,

"Do you know who it is?"

"Gil Walters," they answered.

A hush fell over the crowd. The sheriff dispersed the crowd and called for a wrecker to recover the car. He spoke to Bob about notifying Gil's wife. "I can go see Carol, but you're such good friends, it may be better if you told her. What do you think, Bob?"

"I think you're right. If you don't mind, I'll go by and pick up my wife. Carol may need someone to stay with her tonight."

The sheriff agreed, "That's a good idea, and I'll go by the hospital. We don't want to tell her anything until a doctor has had a look at him. I want to be sure Gil is officially pronounced dead before we do anything. I'll give you a call on the radio."

Bob did not know what to expect inside as they rang the door bell. Word travels fast in a small town, and someone may have already phoned with the news of Gil's death. Carol invited them into a dimly-lit living room. She was dressed in a house robe. Her head was wrapped in a towel which hung over one side of her face. It was obvious she had just gotten out of the shower. There was no indication that she was aware of the accident. She said how nice it was for them to drop by and offered them a cup of tea.

"We're ok, thank you, Carol. I'm afraid I have bad news."

"What do you mean, Bob?"

"Gil was killed tonight in a car wreck east of town. His car went off the road and struck a tree. Bob paused then continued, "They've taken his body to the hospital and are awaiting your instructions as to what you want to do"

Carol said nothing but broke down and began to cry. As Bob's wife consoled her, the towel which had been around Carol's head fell to the floor.

Jane exclaimed, "What has happened to you? Who did this? Did Gil do this to you?" she asked. One side of Carol's face was bruised and badly swollen.

"Yes, he hit me with his fist and kicked me. My side hurts, and I think I may have a broken rib." Bob could not hide his anger. He had felt bad earlier that evening when he remembered how he hated Gil and things he had said about him. He had determined not to think or speak ill of the dead, but after seeing Carol's face, his resolution went out the window. The guilty feeling he had experienced when Gil's death was announced had vanished.

"Get her coat. We're taking her to the hospital."

On the way to the hospital Carol told them that Gil had been drinking and had accused her of an affair. "I thought he was going to kill me."

Bob said without thinking, "If I get my hands on that guy, I'm going to give him a beating he won't forget."

While Carol was being examined, the sheriff told Bob that he was having an autopsy ordered on Gil's body. "I'm also impounding the car for a complete going over. I think it's necessary under the circumstances—you know, because of the nature of Gil's business and all the enemies he had. I just want to be sure this was an accident."

Bob agreed, "I think you're right. I had intended to show you some foot prints around the location where his car left the road, but they were destroyed by all the activity. I saw the same tracks up the road. Perhaps we can go out there later tonight or tomorrow and see if they're still there."

There was plenty of conversation at Don's Café the next day. The news of an autopsy being performed on Gil's body had created much speculation among the town's people. Everyone had a theory. They ranged from accidental death to murder. Hugo had lost many important citizens in the past but, this was different. In this case there was little or no mourning. The greatest emotion seemed to be one of relief. It wasn't that the people wanted Gil dead, but as long as someone had to die, it may as well be him. This would certainly be a major topic of discussion for many months no matter what the results of the investigation revealed.

Bob didn't stop by the café the next morning. He knew what the subject of conversation would be and did not want to get involved. He dropped by later that afternoon for coffee and pie.

Don said, "We missed you this morning. Boy!! You should have been here. The case of Gil's demise was solved several times."

Bob commented, "I'm sure it was. That's why I wasn't here. I didn't want to answer a lot of questions. I told my staff to keep their thoughts on that subject to themselves. I hope they were not involved in any of that crime solving session."

The day of Gil's funeral finally arrived. There had been some delay because of the autopsy. As the hearse made its way through down town, Carol noticed the empty streets when she passed Don's Café. There had been a heavy snow the night before, and a cold wind was blowing. Even so, she thought it strange that no one was seated at the community round table. Surely the regular coffee drinkers and town scholars would not let a little bad weather keep them from exchanging their jokes and solutions of local and world problems. Her thoughts returned to the difficult task facing her. Her husband of three years was to be buried today.

"I wonder how I will react at the church. Will I cry? What will people think if I fail to show sorrow?" She wondered if the black veil would cover the bruises she had received from Gil's last and final beating. "Oh well, no one will be there anyway. Bill and his wife, Bob and Jane will probably be the only ones there. Gil was not well liked to say the least." She recalled how long it had been since she was inside the church. She attended regularly prior to her marriage. To the best of her recollection, it had been about two and a half years. Gil did not think much of the idea of her going to church and would get angry each time she went. When the church was in sight, it was obvious why the streets had been bare. Apparently everyone in town was there. Ushers were telling late comers, "There's standing room only."

Carol did cry that day. She cried not so much for her loss but because of the love, friendship, and understanding being expressed to her. It had been a long time since she had felt those emotions. The people did not like Gil, but they loved Carol and had not been allowed to show it. Hugo had turned out that day in support of Carol.

It was fortunate that district court was just about to get underway. All the personnel and necessary facilities would be available for an immediate hearing. Judge J.P. Carr would preside. "I have a full docket in the weeks ahead, and I would like to complete this preliminary hearing as soon as possible. I don't want any unnecessary delays. Remember this is a hearing so there is no need for formal, long winded speeches." He knew, with a crowed court room, the county attorney would take the opportunity to use his vote getting oratory. "We'll be very informal. Are you ready to present your findings?"

The attorney indicated he was ready and addressed the court to explain the purpose of the hearing and briefly outline the number of witnesses that he expected to testify.

The Judge responded, "Thank you. Call your first witness."

The sheriff was called and sworn in for questioning. "Sheriff, from your notes, and in your own words, describe the events that occurred on the evening of 11 November this year as they relate to the death of Gil Walters."

The sheriff opened his notebook and began, "I was informed by the local police at seven forty five on the evening of 11 November that a wreck had occurred on Highway 70 east of town. A car, which was later determined to belong to Gil Walters, had run off the highway, down an embankment and hit a tree. The paramedic at the scene did a preliminary exam and indicated that no sign of life was apparent. Later at the hospital Doctor Roberts pronounced Gil dead. I impounded the car for investigation and called for an autopsy. The next of kin was notified that evening."

The sheriff paused and sipped from a glass of water before continuing. "I retraced Gil's movements the day of the wreck." The sheriff continued his testimony giving a detailed report of Gil's movements which included time, location, and persons coming in contact with Gil. "The last two persons known to have seen Gil alive were Gary Wallace and Howard Davis." With that statement the sheriff concluded the report of Gil's movements and began to describe the condition of the car.

"The car was checked for fingerprints. None were found that

could not be explained. The front of the car was damaged as you can see in these photos. Notice the windshield is broken on the driver's side. The steering wheel is bent. The left front tire is flat and this is attributed to the collision. There was no indication of a flat from the tire marks on the highway. The right front head light was still on. This aided the rescue party locating the wreck. The brakes appeared to be in working order. As you can see in this picture there was an open can of beer and a fifth of whiskey found in the front floorboard. The beer can was empty and the whiskey bottle was approximately half full. A few articles of clothing were found in the back seat, all of which belonged to Gil."

The sheriff fumbled with his notes then continued, "There was no sign of skidding where the car went over the embankment. There were some footprints in the snow at that location, but they were destroyed by the persons in the recovery party. It is assumed that they belong to the person who called the police department to report the wreck. We have not been able to identify the person who called. We do know it was a woman. The call was probably made from the pay phone outside the Cottonwood Club."

"That is all I have to report on the investigation except I was notified that Dr. Johnson had completed the autopsy last week. He will give the coroner's report." The county attorney dismissed the sheriff, but he was subject to recall.

"I call Gary Wallace to the witness stand."

"Mr. Wallace, did you meet with Mr. Gil Walters on the afternoon of 11 November this year?"

"Yes, I did."

"Tell the court the circumstance surrounding that meeting."

"He came by my garage around two o'clock that afternoon. He had been drinking and was obnoxious as usual. He said there was a leak in the brake lines and wanted it fixed. I told him to take it somewhere else that I didn't have time to fix it. Then he pulled that tough guy routine on me and said he would be back in two hours, and the leak better be fixed. He also made a comment about my sixteen year old daughter. After that comment, I wasn't about to fix his brakes. He left his car parked in front with the keys in the ignition. He came back around four or five o'clock, got in the car, and drove off. I'm sure he thought I had worked on his car. I didn't have time to tell him that I had not fixed the brakes. I'm not sure I would have even if I had had the opportunity. That was the last I saw of him."

"My next witness is Howard Davis." Before Howard could make his way to the stand the Judge tugged at his stomach and called a fifteen minute break.

"We will get to Mr. Davis when we resume."

After the break, Howard began his testimony. "Gil arrived at my place around six fifteen that evening. The attorney interrupted and asked Howard to identify "his place." I own the Cottonwood Club. I had not opened yet. He knocked on the front door for a few minutes, but when I didn't open up, he came through the side door. He was about three sheets in the wind." The attorney stopped Howard again and asked him to explain what he meant by three sheets in the wind. "It means drunk. Everybody knows that! As I was saying, he came in the side door and began to question me about Carol's visits. I told him she had been here earlier but had been gone two or three hours. He was mad that she had been visiting. She visits mostly with my wife. Of course Gil tried to make something nasty out of it. As if Carol would have anything to do with an old—aaah—fellow like me. We are friends, and that's all. He told me if I didn't put a stop to it I might find my place burned to the ground with me and mine in it. He grabbed the can of beer I had sitting on the bar and stormed out the door. I had put some sedative in that beer, but I didn't tell him. Then he left and I was glad to see him go. That was around six thirty. I know because I was just about ready to open up."

This was new information to the attorney. "Why on earth did you put sedative in the beer, Howard?"

"Everybody knows my old tom cat. He's really not mine, but he hangs around the place. He goes out tom-cat'n around at night and gets into fights with other tom cats, I suppose. He came out on the short end of the stick and was chewed up bad. He's wild as a March hare so, I decided to put sedative in his nightly beer. I figured it's the only way I could catch him to take him to the vet. He's a good mouser, and I would hate to lose him. I was just about to pour it in the cat's bowl when Gil came in."

"Why didn't you tell Gil there was sedative in the beer?"

"Well, I would have if I could have stopped him or if he had offered to pay for it. That was stealing as for as I'm concerned. I worried about it for a minute or so, and then figured that sleep might the best thing for him in his condition. If that had anything to do with the wreck, I'm sorry."

"What kind of sedative did you put in the beer, Howard?"

Howard reached into his pocket, "It's a prescription my wife has for sleeping.

I have the bottle here. You can see it." He gave the prescription bottle to the attorney and started to leave the witness stand.

"One more question before you're through, Howard. Did you see anyone in or near the pay phone outside your club the evening of 11 November?"

"No. I didn't" replied Howard.

"Thank you. That will be all. You can sit down."

The next testimony was what everyone was waiting for, the coroner's report.

"Gil Walters died from a severe blow on the head. There were cuts about the face and neck. Glass from the windshield was embedded in the head wound and face. There were bruises around the chest and shoulder area. There was internal damage, but the cause of death was the head trauma." Dr. Johnson presented photographs and x-rays to the court showing the injuries he was describing. He stated the alcohol content of his blood was well over the amount to be considered intoxicated. Estimated time of death was between six and seven o'clock. "The injuries are consistent with those I have seen in the past resulting from the head on collision of two automobiles."

The county attorney continued, "Take a look at this prescription for sedatives and tell the court if you are familiar with this drug." Dr. Johnson indicated he had prescribed that drug many times and was familiar with its effects. The doctor was asked, "How quick does the drug take affect? Would the test you did on Gil's blood check for drugs of this type?"

After a moment's pause the Doctor answered, "The drug's effect would vary with each person and situation. I can't give you a time. Yes, the test I ran on Gil's blood would indicate the presence of this drug if it was there."

The attorney approached the witness and asked, "Was there any presence of this drug or any other?" That question created a stir throughout the court room.

"No, there was not." The sigh of relief coming from Howard Davis could be heard throughout the halls of the old court house.

After conferring with the sheriff, the attorney told the judge he had an additional witness. It would be the last witness to be called, but he was not in court.

"The sheriff can have him here in fifteen minutes if we have a recess."

The judge agreed to break for lunch, reconvene at one thirty, and the witness would be heard at that time. The missing witness turned out to be John Allen who worked at the A-1 Brake Service Company. The attorney started his questioning,

"Mr. Allen, it is my understanding that you checked the brakes on the wrecked automobile which belonged to Gil Walters. Is that correct?"

"Yes I did", replied John.

"Did you check the level of the brake fluid?"

"Yes, it was low, but the brakes were still in working order. There was enough fluid to pressure up the system."

"Thank you. You can get back to work, and I appreciate you getting here on such short notice." The county attorney concluded, "Your Honor, that's all of the testimony we have to present. Do you have any further questions?"

The judge rubbed his chin, leaned back in his chair, and looked as if he were in deep thought. He told the attorney to approach the bench. "I was wondering why you didn't call Carol Walters as a witness." The attorney explained that he and the sheriff had questioned her thoroughly and felt that she could add nothing new to the investigation. He indicated they didn't want to put her through any more stress but offered to call her. "No, I don't think it's necessary. Take your seat." the judge answered.

Addressing the entire court the judge stated, "I believe it's very clear that this was an accident. An accident with extenuating circumstances, that is, since there was alcohol involved. But, none-the-less, an accidental death, and that's my ruling. Gil Walters's death is ruled accidental. I cannot close this hearing without saying this. Howard Davis, you better be more careful about that tomcat's beer. You were lucky that Gil did not drink any of it. If that sedative had shown up in his blood, we could be seeing a lot of each other. This hearing is adjourned."

There was little excitement around town, and time seemed to drag. The winter weather was unusually cold and wet. There had been several snow and ice storms. During those periods very few people went outside unless it was absolutely necessary. Bob and his staff were busy helping those who had to travel. They often checked on the elderly to see that they had heat and ample food.

"Here's the list of persons to check on. I want you to phone or go by at least every other day when there is snow or ice on the roads. Mrs. Land will be called every day. I sure don't want her on the roads in bad weather. She does enough damage when it's clear. I should call her insurance agent and have him check, he has the most to lose." Bob instructed. Everyone was looking forward to spring.

Carol was busy getting her late husband's business dealings settled. There was a life insurance claim to process and paperwork to complete the sale of Gil's three taverns. She had indicated to the realtor, "There is no way I will be directly or indirectly involved with the operation of those taverns. I'll accept any reasonable offer just short of giving them away." The realtor did a good job and had received fair offers on all three taverns from Gil's former employees. Carol was pleased that the weather had prohibited travel. She was not ready to visit and needed a little more time to adjust to her new situation. Bob and Jane and a few of her close friends had dropped by to see if she needed anything. They did not stay long, and that was fine with Carol.

Winter was just about over and everyone was moving about town doing the things they had been unable to do for months. Gardeners were breaking ground for the upcoming season. City road workers were busy repairing damage created by the cold weather. Shops were displaying bathing suits and outdoor sportswear. Members of the Chamber of Commerce were planning the town's annual 4th of July picnic. It was as if the town had awakened from a deep sleep. Carol had even begun to venture outside. This presented a problem for deputy Hank Green because he wanted to ask Carol for a date but thought it might be too soon after Gil's death. He knew there would be others wanting to invite her out, and he wanted to be first. He decided he would ask Bob for guidance and to lead interference for him. Bob told him he would be talking to Carol often, and he would let him know when the time was right. He continued, "You better be nice to her, and you know what I mean. She is not going to be just another notch on your gun. If you hurt her, I will string you up by your toes. When you ask her out the first time I suggest you invite her to church. Next, you might ask her to dinner." Bob grinned and said," If she hasn't become tired of you by then, you could suggest a movie or something. I think that would be a good start."

This was not what Hank had in mind but agreed that he would follow his advice and assured Bob that he was serious about her. "You know how I have always felt about her. I had a few dates with her before she was married. I was not ready or prepared for a serious relationship at that time. It was only after she got married that I realized how much she meant to me."

At Jane's urging, Bob had spoken with Carol several times during the past few weeks. At first he and Jane were pleased with the progress she was making putting her life back in order. Carol had done a magnificent job handling the business side of her life. Now it was time to work on the social aspects. This would be more difficult for her, and she would need a push. Bob said, "Jane wants to go shopping in Oklahoma City but I don't want her to go alone. She saw a dress advertised that she thinks she can't live without. Would you go with her? You might find something you like as well." Bob knew if anything would get a woman out of the house, it would be an opportunity to go shopping.

"Yes, I think I would enjoy taking a trip with Jane. When does she plan on going?"

Bob did not know what Jane had planned for the next few days, but he had to say something "As soon as you can go. She is ready anytime. I'll have her call you to set the date." Bob felt good that the plan was working. He would drive directly to his house and tell Jane. Knowing how his wife liked to travel and shop, he was sure she would go along with the arrangement.

Jane and Carol had completed a very successful day and half of shopping in the big city. They had just returned to their hotel room to check out when the phone rang. It was a call from Bob,

"I want you to stay an extra night. We've had our usual late winter snowstorm, and the roads are bad. I think they'll be clear by tomorrow afternoon. I'll call tomorrow and let you know if it's ok to travel. I'm sure it's breaking your heart to have another half day to shop, but you'll just have to grin and bare it."

As expected the roads were clear, and the pair returned home safely the following afternoon. Jane was anxious to model her new dress for Bob, "I know I spent more for this than I should have, but isn't it just right for church and special occasions? Remember, it was your idea for me to go shopping."

Bob smiled, "I remember. That's ok. You look beautiful."

Jane was pleased with Bob's comment and continued, "Carol bought several outfits. Just wait till you see her! She's a new woman!"

Bob was seated at his desk when he saw Carol go by the window. She was on her way to pay her bill at the water department. He waited for her to return and went outside to invite her in for a cup of their famous coffee. He was disappointed that she was not dressed in one of her new outfits. "I thought that you would be showing off your new clothes." Carol informed Bob that men didn't know anything about women's apparel.

"The things I bought were for summer and early fall. Besides, I'm not going to take a chance on ruining my new wardrobe in this messy weather. Carol refused the coffee saying that she had heard about their coffee and didn't care to be sleepless for a week.

On the way to Carol's car, Bob informed her, "That's why I have my coffee at Don's." Carol had parked in an area that had a thin layer of snow remaining on the sidewalk. They made their parting comments, and Carol drove away. Turning to go back to his office Bob looked down at the sidewalk, and there it was. A footprint with a triangular shaped logo on the heel that was clear as day and a grooved cut near the big toe area of the left foot.

Thoughts were racing through Chief Baker's mind, "I saw those same footprints in the snow the night Gil died. No mistake about it, she was there. Should I confront her? No, I think justice was served. I'll leave it that way. I prefer a system of justice to a legal system any day. Everyone in town feels the same. Still, I sure would like to know what really happened out there that night. Maybe someday I'll ask."

CHAPTER 2

All's fair in Love and Horses

EVERY SUMMER SEVERAL YOUNG PEOPLE WOULD COME TO HUGO FOR a visit with friends or kinfolk. Soon the visitors were involved in all the youth activities around town. It was exciting meeting kids from other schools, and it would not be long before good friendships developed. Problems arose from time to time, but they were usually resolved to everyone's satisfaction.

Take the case of Billy Smith and Jimmy Lang. Jimmy was visiting for the summer. He became infatuated with a local girl named Barbara. The visitor gave his very best effort to let her know how he felt. She did not respond in a positive way, but didn't discourage him either. That presented a problem for the local boy. Billy had been dating her for several weeks. They had no arrangement to go steady, but they seemed to enjoy being together. He was very fond of her and hoped that something more permanent would develop.

There was a square dance scheduled for Friday night and both boys had intentions of asking Barbara to be their date. Jimmy told Billy that he was wasting his time asking Barbara.

"You know she would prefer to go with me," Jimmy announced.

"I don't know about that. We'll let her decide. I'm sure I'll be swinging her around the dance floor come Friday night," Billy replied.

Jimmy said, "There's a way we could settle this and save all of us a lot of trouble. You and I could have a race and the winner would get a clear field. The loser gets out of the picture completely. Do you have enough guts to race?"

"What kind of race do you propose?" Billy asked.

"I thought we could have a horse race. There are plenty of horses around here, surely we could borrow two," he answered. Jimmy thought he could outride anyone in town because he was a member of an equestrian club in Oklahoma City. He would have an unfair advantage but that's what he wanted.

"I'll borrow two horses. You can have your choice, but I get to say where we race," Billy responded after some careful thought. Billy didn't really want to race, but he was not positive that Barbara would prefer a country boy, like himself, over a suave and debonair big city dude.

"We'll race to that post about three hundred yards away. You see the one I'm talking about? That post in-line with those cows. This road goes right by it. You see it? The first one to touch the post wins," Billy stated the rules of the race.

"Yes. Yes, I see it. I'll take this horse," Jimmy said. Actually the choice of horses was not difficult. One horse was a beautiful bay and the other was a swayback nag that looked as if it couldn't run one hundred yards much less three hundred.

"This is going to be a piece of cake," Jimmy thought.

Although Jimmy was sure of a win he asked Billy's friend, Steve, "Is it necessary to stay on the road?"

"He didn't say anything about how you get there. I guess you could go in a straight line near those cows and have a shorter distance. It would be thirty or forty yards shorter, I think," Steve answered.

The race was on. Billy headed down the road while Jimmy took off in a straight line for the finish. It was not going to be much of a race after all. Bill's horse was in a slow trot while Jimmy's was flying at top speed. Yes, it was a piece of cake, that is, until Jimmy neared the cattle. The sound of the approaching horse scared the cows, and they scattered. Jimmie's horse made a quick ninety degree turn and took after one of the cows that strayed from the herd. Jimmy became airborne and continued toward the finish. After all, his intentions were to travel in a straight line. He made a graceful landing, slid about five yards, only bouncing two or three times before coming to a complete stop. In the meantime Billy circled the finish line and was headed back to declare himself the winner.

Billy and Barbara were promenading in fine fashion at the Friday night square dance when Jimmy arrived and joined Steve in the stag line.

"Don't they make a fine looking couple?" Steve asked.

"Yea, yea, I don't see what she sees in that dumb character. I still don't know how he could have won that race. Everything was against him. I had the better horse. I took the shortest path. He was too dumb to figure that out.

Steve thought to himself "Yes, he was dumb. He knew you would take the shortest route by the cattle. Because you're a smart guy and would want every advantage. He also knew you wouldn't choose the sway back horse. You have a better eye for horses than that. He knew that the cattle would scatter when you approached them at full speed. But the dumbest thing he did was to let you choose his dad's champion cutting horse."

CHAPTER 3

Saturday's Hero

THE DOWNTOWN STREETS AND SIDEWALKS OF HUGO WERE ALWAYS crowded on Saturdays. That was the day everyone set aside for shopping. This was particularly true for those living outside the city. Farmers from the surrounding area would arrive early in their horse-drawn wagons. There were several vacant lots near downtown where they parked. The wagons would serve as a meeting point for the family during the day. They traveled back and forth between chores. Groceries, clothes, haircuts, farm equipment, and getting their horses shod were items normally found on their shopping list. Everyone enjoyed visiting with those they had not seen since the previous Saturday. Store clerks would be busy ringing up sales. Although the stores and sidewalks were crowded, no one seemed to be in a hurry. Waiting in line for service was an opportunity to discuss subjects like Becky's new baby or the best crop to plant next spring. It was a typical summer Saturday in Hugo.

There were several things to do for entertainment after completing their shopping. Going to one of the three movie theaters was almost compulsory. A few cars and pick-ups filled with noisy teens heading to their favorite swimming hole could be seen traveling through downtown. One hardware store was located near a wagon parking lot. The owner provided several tables just outside his building. These tables were used for various purposes, but the most popular activity was checkers.

My friend Red worked for the owner Saturday afternoons. He was hired to play checkers, and take on all comers. Men would line up to see if they could outwit the young sixth grader. Many tried. Few succeeded. My buddy had an uncanny knowledge of the game. He was paid twenty-five cents per hour. This was good wages for the times. It was profitable venture for the store owner too. He would pay Red seventy five cents for three hours work. The profit from hardware sold to the men who gathered to watch and play far exceeded Red's salary.

During the evening hours many of the grown-ups would park their cars in front of the downtown businesses to watch and visit with people walking by. Young kids would run up and down the sidewalks playing. Men would generally stand in front of their car and engage those passing in conversation. The women would remain in the car. If there were ladies walking by they would be directed to the car. "Have a chat with the wife." they would say. This may seem like dull entertainment, but everyone had a great time. The topics discussed had no limit. This was prior to the invention of television and its debilitating effect on the art of conversation.

Occasionally, someone would beat Red; the victor would travel the entire street explaining every move he had made with the checkers. He would receive hand shakes, congratulations, and pats on the back. You would have thought he had hit the home run to win the World Series. I couldn't understand how so much pride of winning could result from a grown man defeating an eleven year old boy. He was definitely Saturday's hero.

CHAPTER 4

Time goes by

THEY SAY THAT TIME PASSES FASTER AS YOU GROW OLDER, AND I WOULD agree. Comparing two Christmas Eve nights from different periods of my life would certainly bear that out. As a young boy, my mother would tuck me into bed with a final comment,

"Go to sleep now. We have a big day ahead of us, tomorrow will be Christmas!" That declaration was unnecessary! My brother and I had been sneaking around looking for gifts in closets and other potential hiding places for weeks. In all our attempts I cannot remember one successful search.

The temperature in our bedroom was cold, and the warmth of the down cover felt good. Most nights I would have been asleep in minutes, but not this night. The minutes seemed like hours, and hours seemed like days. I was afraid I would be too old for my gifts by the time morning arrived. After what I felt was a reasonable time, I would ask, "Daddy, is it time yet?"

He would reply, "No son, not yet."

This exchange would occur several times during the night until finally he agreed that, "Yes, son, it's time."

We were not allowed to go into the living room where the Christmas tree and stockings were until we had fully dressed, and the chill of the night air had warmed. Soon dad had a fire built in the fireplace, and all was ready for our much-anticipated entrance. I'm not sure what time we got up on those mornings. Judging the length of time before daylight after we had opened our gifts, it must have been around five a.m. As I look back on those days, I marvel at my Dad's patience and understanding.

Years later when our daughter was four years old, my wife and I purchased a doll house for her Christmas present. It was Christmas Eve, and all were in bed except my wife and me. It was time to place Santa's gifts under the tree. Several times my wife told me that I had better prepare the doll house. Feeling confident that it would be an easy task, I waited until ten thirty before moving to the garage to begin. The package was marked, "Some Assembly Required". Upon opening the box, much to my surprise, none of the parts were assembled. I organized the various pieces and started fitting the parts together.

The progress was going amazingly well. The job was about seventy-five per cent complete, and the time was one a.m. My wife said she was going to bed since she could be of little or no help. I was pleased with myself especially since the work had been accomplished without referring to the instructions once. As the last portion of the outer wall was placed, I discovered there was a part left over.

Retrieving the instructions from the waste basket, I determined that the extra part was an interior wall. The entire project would have to be disassembled. To make matters worse I found that a part was missing.

Luckily, a sheet of aluminum material was available and suitable for making the missing part. I worked feverishly cutting, painting, and assembling parts. At each stage I would check the clock and wonder where the time went. The hours seemed like minutes, the minutes like seconds. Would there be enough time?

The project was finished, and I had just laid my head on the pillow when I heard a familiar refrain, "Daddy, is it time yet?"

CHAPTER 5

Two Black Marks

THE MOST EXCITING MOMENT IN A YOUNG PERSON'S LIFE IS NOT THE final bell of the school year, the first kiss, or even winning the big game. The most exciting event is—getting one's driver's license!! No longer suffering the embarrassment of being chauffeured by a parent does wonders for your self esteem. That feeling of independence and freedom is overwhelming.

I remember the day my brother took the test. He had made a good grade on the written portion during the morning session. Driving would be evaluated that afternoon. My brother and the driving evaluator got in the car and took off. Having traveled less than two hundred feet my brother was told to return to the office. He had failed. It would be another week before he could retake the test.

"You had two black marks," the evaluator commented.

Several times my brother retraced his actions but could not determine what he had done to receive two black marks. "Did I not signal? I didn't change lanes so that couldn't be the problem. Oh well, I'll just show him my best driving skills." he thought.

The following week, once again, he traveled less than two hundred feet before being told to return to the office.

"You had two black marks," the observer commented.

He was not going another week without knowing what he was doing wrong. "I can't figure out what I did to get two black marks. Won't you tell me what it is so I can correct it?" he asked.

"Go outside and look around. I think you will be able to figure it out,"

He looked for traffic signs—there were none. Traffic lanes—there were none.

"What could it be?" He spent several minutes studying the area. Suddenly the answer was there!!

The following week he passed his driving test with flying colors. That day Joel learned a valuable lesson—you don't burn rubber when taking a driving test.

It leaves two black marks!

CHAPTER 6

Bumper Cars

HUGO'S CHIEF OF POLICE BOB BAKER HAD JUST RECEIVED HIS NEW patrol car. It had colorful markings unlike chief's cars in the past. He was very proud and was driving around town showing it to anyone who would take the time to look. Bob was on his way to the office when he saw Mrs. Land coming from the opposite direction several blocks away. Mrs. Land was a sweet elderly lady who had lived in Hugo all of her life. She had a standing order with the car dealer for a new red Oldsmobile every two years. Her driving ability was well known throughout town, and everyone recognized her red car immediately.

She was short of stature and even though she had pillows in the driver's seat, her view of the road was through the steering wheel. It appeared at times that there was no driver at all. Her top speed was less than twenty five miles per hour. To a stranger, it looked as if an empty car was rolling slowly down the street.

As the cars were approaching one another, Bob pulled over to the curb and came to a complete stop. He felt helpless as he watched the Oldsmobile glance off his new front left fender. After the initial shock and a brief moment of anger passed, he got out on the passenger side to look at the condition of the cars. There was not much damage since

Mrs. Land was in the process of braking at the time of the collision. Mrs. Land remained seated while Bob did the inspection.

Bob reported, “It looks like you and I are going to be visiting the body shop tomorrow.”

Mrs. Land kept repeating, “It was my fault. It was my fault.”

Bob assured her it was not her fault.

“No. It was my fault, Chief Baker”.

Bob replied, “No, Mrs. Land, it was my fault. I saw you coming three blocks away and had two opportunities to turn off, and I didn’t. It was my fault. Now, you go home and drive real careful.”

As Bob continued driving to the office, he laughed and thought how much he loved this town and the people in it.

CHAPTER 7

Old Friends

It was nearing time for homecoming, and there were several former Hugo graduates in town to plan reunion activities. The various class committees would make arrangements for food, entertainment, and meeting places. Of course there would be visits to the high school and special dinners for each graduating class. Tim Randolph and Gary Wallace were seated at Don's Cafe when Tim looked out the window and exclaimed, "Well bless my soul. Here comes FiFi"!!!

"Who is FiFi?" Gary said while glancing outside to see a very attractive woman headed toward the door.

"I'll tell you later. And don't mention that name to her." Tim met her at the door and it was obvious that they were very pleased to see each other. After a hug and few comments about how well each looked, Tim brought her to the table for introductions.

"Gary Wallace, I would like you to meet Sue, a dear friend and former classmate. She is on our class reunion planning committee this year. We went all the way through school together from the first grade to graduation. Proud Class of '39. Isn't that right, Sue?"

"Yes I've had to put up with this guy all these years. What's amazing, I still like him. Although at times it has been difficult. I knew I would find you sitting down drinking coffee. Gary, have you ever actually seen him do any work around this town?"

Gary smiled and said, "Not often."

They continued to talk about Hugo, old times, and changes that had been made since Sue's last visit. "Speaking of changes, I had better get to my garage and see what changes are taking place there. It was very nice meeting you." Gary left Sue and Tim laughing and enjoying each other's company. Gary thought there must be a good story there. He could hardly wait to hear more about the good looking woman called FiFi.

It was several days before Tim and Gary were alone to continue their conversation.

Gary said "I can't wait any longer. You've got to tell me about FiFi."

"It was just after Christmas when we were in the fifth grade. We were back in school for the first time since the holidays. Sue's family was better off financially than most. She had received a watch and perfume from Santa Clause. Times were hard, and this was much more than the rest of us kids had received. Her parents told her not to say anything about her gifts. This would be difficult. She wore her watch and would hold it to her ear and listen to the ticking every few minutes. She offered to let several listen to the beautiful ticking of her watch, but everyone refused. The fragrance of her perfume could be detected over a distance of several feet. Not one person mentioned the pleasant odor. Being ignored was too much for her to take. She asked the teacher if she could make an announcement to the class. Of course the teacher did not know what she was going to say but agreed and called the class to attention.

Sue got in front of the class and said 'If you hear anything today, it's me. If you smell anything today, it's me too.'

Well, of course, you know what we thought. The class liked to have killed ourselves laughing. It took ten minutes for the teacher to gain control of the class.

The teacher left the room at one point. I don't know why, but I suspect she had trouble keeping a straight face and did not want us to see her break up. The rest of the day there were spontaneous outburst of laughter and giggles. Some of the boys would repeat her speech, with sound effects added. This would disrupt the entire class. I think about a third of the boys were sent to the principal's office before the day was over.

She got the nickname FiFi over the incident. After a period of time no one outside of our class knew what the nickname was about, and she actually began to like it. However, I would not call her that today. I'm careful not to mention her perfume, and I would never ask her what time it is."

CHAPTER 8

First Impression

Bob and Betty Albert were making a final check of the house. They were expecting their new preacher and his wife this morning. Wanting to make a good impression, they had thoroughly cleaned. The timing of the new pastor's visit was good since they had just bought new carpet and living room furniture.

"Come in and welcome," Betty greeted. As she opened the door wide, a cute little dog ran inside and jumped on the couch. "I'm John Simpson, and this is my wife, Mary. We spoke on the phone about a get acquainted meeting this morning. I hope we are not inconveniencing you."

"Not at all, we were expecting you and looking forward to our meeting. Please come into the living room, and we can talk," Betty answered. John took a seat in a chair facing the couch. The little dog immediately jumped into his lap. After petting the dog he gently placed the dog on the floor. It was apparent that the dog was shedding. There were several hairs left on John's freshly cleaned and pressed suit.

Mary told Betty she liked their house and the furniture was arranged wonderfully.

"I wish I had your skill in decorating," she added.

After a few exchanges regarding furniture arranging, Betty asked,

"Would you care for coffee or tea and homemade cookies?" John and Mary indicated they would love to have coffee and one of her cookies. Betty attended to the refreshments in the kitchen while Bob continued their conversation.

"Have you gotten settled in town yet? Moving can be nerve racking. I would hate to think of moving with all the stuff we've accumulated over the years. We've lived in this house for thirty five years."

"Oh, yes. Of course, we still have some things in storage but we're making progress. We really do like the town and everyone has been very helpful." Mary answered.

John asked, "How long have you and Betty been members of the church?"

"I think Betty was born in the church. I was joking. She has been attending all her life. I didn't move here until I was a freshman in high school. My family and I joined the first Sunday we were in town. Let's see, that would be almost forty two years ago."

Betty returned with coffee and a platter of cookies. "I hope you like oatmeal cookeeeee!" About the time she finished her sentence the dog tripped her and she dumped the tray of coffee and cookies on the couch. The dog immediately began to eat the cookies that spilled on the carpet.

Betty ran to the kitchen for a towel while Bob got the vacuum and began to clean the cookie crumbs. Having blotted the coffee and cleared the remaining cookies, Betty said, "I'm afraid that was all the coffee and cookies. I had no idea that dog was at my feet. I hope I didn't kick him too hard." She was obviously upset.

John whispered to Mary, "Maybe we had better leave. I don't think this is a good time to continue our visit." John announced that they had to go. He explained their next appointment was across town, and they would need extra time to find the location.

Bob and Betty escorted John and Mary to the door. The little dog followed tugging at John's trousers all the way to the porch. As they were about to say good bye John asked, "What is your dog's name?

"Our dog!! That's not our dog! We thought it was your dog!" Bob exclaimed.

"No. He was on your porch when we came, and we just assumed he was yours." Mary chimed in.

"This is terrible. We did so want to make a good first impression. I'm afraid your short visit has been anything but that. I'm sure you wondered why we would let a dog get hair all over your suit. Not even correcting the dog!" Betty said with a crack in her voice as if she were about to cry.

"And I'm sure you were wondering why we would bring a dog on a visit. Not only that but allowing it to jump on your nice furniture. You must have thought we were very inconsiderate." John replied.

After a moment's silence, John suggested that they try to forget their meeting and start over. "First impressions are not always that important. If we can start over and look on the humorous side of this visit, I think we are going to be very good friends." They did, and they were, for many years.

The uninvited guest from next door

CHAPTER 9

First Love

Today will be an important day in Menda's life. She and her best friend, Flonnie, will be making another trip to Gray's drug store where Bill, her true love, works behind the soda fountain. She had made several trips to see him in the past month. Although there had been little or no conversation between them, she knew that he must have strong feelings for her. Menda said, "I know the signs to look for since I read the latest issue of "Young Romances". Besides, women just know those things." Each and every time she had entered the store, she was greeted with his infectious smile and comment, "How can I help you ladies today?" She liked the term "ladies" used in his greeting. It was a term generally used for older, mature women. The fact that Menda was in junior high and Bill was in Hugo High obviously didn't matter to him. "True love can overcome an age difference. He is just wonderful," she thought.

Why would today's visit be different from others in the past? Today Bill would be given an opportunity to express his true feelings to Menda. The school yearbooks had been distributed. Menda and the other students were busy collecting signatures and expressions of thought from their fellow students. She would present her book to Bill and ask him to write something. He would not even have to utter a word aloud. That might be easier since they hadn't verbally stated their affection for one another.

As Menda and Flonnie entered the drug store, they were greeted with the usual phrase. They ordered ice cream cones and sat at a table near the soda fountain. When Bill delivered the ice cream, Menda noticed that she had been given a slightly larger dip than her friend. "Just another sign," she thought. She asked if he would write something in her year book. He agreed. Menda showed him a space to write at the back of her book. She did not want his writing near others, since it would be more private and personal.

"What would he write? Ask me for a date, maybe. Go steady? Maybe, it's possible. Proposal of marriage would be out of the question since he was so young. I don't know what he will write except I know it will be very romantic." These thoughts were racing through Menda's mind. Bill returned the book and said, "I hope you enjoyed the ice cream." They assured him they had and left the store immediately.

Flonnie wanted to see what he had written, but Menda refused to allow anyone to read it before she had scrutinized every word looking for possible hidden meanings. Only then, would she allow her best friend to read his writings. Menda had decided to wait until she arrived at home before looking. She went directly to her room and slowly opened the book and began to read:

"There was a boy
named Johnny McGuire
Who ran down the street
with his britches on fire.
He ran to the doctor
and fainted from fright
When the doctor told him
his end was in sight."

Best wishes, Bill

Johnny McGuire's was not the only end in sight. There was an immediate reduction in ice cream sales at Gray's Drug.

CHAPTER 10

Here Comes the Judge

HUGO WAS THE COUNTY SEAT OF CHOCTAW COUNTY AND HAD A beautiful old court house in which to conduct the legal business of the county and state. The front of the building had large columns with several steps leading up to the main entrance. There were marble steps and wooden paneling throughout the three stories. The inside of the building showed signs of wear, but one could tell that no expense had been spared when the structure was built. There were several court rooms, judge's chambers, and sheriff's offices on the second and third floors. The first floor had a snack bar right next to the offices where excited sixteen year old kids could take the drivers license exam. The court house grounds consisted of a city block and were very well maintained. There were a variety of flowers, shrubs, and large trees with several benches scattered around for people to rest and enjoy the surroundings.

The park-like atmosphere on the outside was in sharp contrast to many of the activities conducted on the inside. District court was about to begin and summonses had been mailed to citizens for jury selection. Jim Sanders, Gary Wallace and Tim Randolph were having coffee at Don's Café when Jim said, "Tim, I thought you were called for jury duty. How did you get out of it?"

"I didn't!! What time is it? Oooooh, I'm an hour late, I'll see you guys," Tim answered as he ran out the door.

The jury selection process was underway when he entered the courtroom. When Judge Davis saw Tim arrive, he stopped the proceedings and asked him to come before the court. The Judge and Tim were good friends. Their families frequently had dinner together, and they had played golf in the same foursome each week end for several years.

"Good morning, Mr. Randolph."

"Good morning, J.P."

The Judge responded, "You will address me as Judge Davis or Your Honor when you are before this court. Now, I suppose you were sick this morning, and that is why you were late reporting. Isn't that right?"

"No, Judge Davis, I'm feeling fine."

Again the Judge asked, "Well, then I suppose Mary was sick, and you had to care of her. Isn't that correct?"

"No, Your Honor, she is feeling fine, too."

"Well, then your car must not have been running, and you had to get a ride with someone else. Isn't that right?"

"No, Your Honor, that old Ford is running like a top."

The Judge looked disgusted and slammed his gavel down, "Twenty dollar fine for contempt of court! You'll learn to be here on time. You can pay the clerk later. Now, be seated with the rest of the jury pool, and we will get on with the selection." As Tim slithered into a seat, there were muffled sounds of laughter coming from the audience. The judge addressed the lawyers, "Let's get on with this. I want twelve good jurors, and I don't want to take all day selecting them."

Tim was not selected for a jury and was dismissed for the remainder of the day. He was instructed to be back in court the following morning at eight o'clock.

The next day he arrived early. That afternoon he was in Don's Café when J.P. walked by and saw Tim sitting at the front table.

J.P. went inside, "I noticed you arrived on time this morning."

Tim replied, "Yeah, I didn't want another round like I had yesterday. Twenty dollars is pretty steep. You didn't give me a chance to tell you why I was late."

"I guess you're right. But I gave you three chances for an excuse that I could accept and you were too dumb to take them. Come by my chambers tomorrow, and I will have the court recorder enter your reason for being late. Then I will cancel that fine. You know I can't show favoritism in front of everybody. I just didn't want you to come out with something idiotic or stupid like: "I was having coffee at Don's Café and forgot." By the way, what was your reason for being late?"

"I'll pay the fine."

CHAPTER 11

Home Cooking

For most people the phrase "home cooking" triggers thoughts of wonderful meals, featuring those special dishes that only your mother could prepare. Good memories of the perfectly baked turkey, biscuits, cake, etc. are supposed to set the standard by which you measure taste. However, I have a slightly different outlook regarding that term. When I was young, having a meal at my house was special, but not because of the food. It was a time for all to share the events of the day or plan for the future. Happy conversation, that's what I remember when I hear the words "home cooking".

I loved my mother very much, but to be honest she was definitely not a gourmet cook. She used two settings on her stove; off and high. I'm amused when I see menu items today described as Cajun blackened ; as if the Cajuns invented that method of cooking. Most dishes my mother cooked were blackened. She was aware of her inabilities as a cook and joked about it frequently. When I got married, mother told my wife there was one thing she would never have to worry about. She would never have to listen to me say, "This dish isn't as good as my mother's." For the most part that has proven to be true since my wife is an excellent cook.

However, there were some dishes mother cooked that deserve

honorable mention. Her dressing, fried chicken, cornbread, and enchiladas were perfect. Although no one in the family could understand these phenomena, we did recognize her expertise preparing those dishes. I don't think mother understood it either, but she took great pleasure serving these items. Aside from the four culinary delights, most of her remaining entrees had a definite burnt or charcoal taste. It wasn't until I left home that I realized there were more than three or four flavors in food.

Her most unique preparation was "made-from-scratch drop biscuits." Each biscuit had two or three little spikes on top. As the biscuits cooked, the spike would brown and harden. If you patted the biscuit with the palm of your hand, it would stick you. It was necessary to remove the "fangs" before taking the first bite, or it would bite back. When I saw a full pan of her biscuits, I visualized a bed of nails.

Mother's greatest cooking triumph and disaster occurred while preparing the same meal. She was serving the annual family Thanksgiving dinner. Several members of the family arrived early to assist mother. The meal was to be served at two o'clock. Various jobs were assigned, and all seemed to be coming together nicely. Shortly before the scheduled time to remove the turkey, it was discovered she had failed to turn the oven on!!!!!

Three hours later, when everyone was nearly starved, we sat down for what was the best—tasting meal we had ever eaten. Mother had learned the secret to good cooking. Delay long enough, and everything tastes wonderful. The meal was a success, and all had a great time. Years have passed, and mother is no longer with us. The taste standards set in my early years have changed for the most part. But I would give almost anything to sit down to one more of mother's over-cooked and blackened meals. By the way, I still like lumps in my cream of wheat.

CHAPTER 12

The Way You Say It

WHEN DOROTHY FRENCH WAS ATTENDING HUGO HIGH SCHOOL, SHE lived in the country with her grandfather and aunt. Her family was poor, and they had rough times just getting by. Each morning she would walk a distance of one mile to catch a school bus. If it rained, the dirt road would be muddy. She would take her shoes off and walk barefoot. Well water was available at the bus stop, and she would wash the mud off her feet before the school bus arrived.

Her clothes were home-made. They were always clean, but the style was not up to the standards of those kids who lived in town. They had store-bought clothes. Dorothy was a very proud person, and although some looked down on her, she did not share that opinion. She would not accept the notion that she was less a person for being poor. Dorothy never met anyone that she thought was better than she. By the same token she was never better than others. It was an even playing field, as far as she was concerned. Probably because of this attitude, she had many friends and was not mistreated by her fellow classmates. This cannot be said about one of her teachers.

Dorothy's home economics teacher had made several derogatory comments about all the kids who lived in the country. They were hopelessly lacking in grace and charm. The teacher never passed up an opportunity to prove her bigoted point of view. One day she was describing the proper manners to follow while attending an elegant breakfast. She said, "Dorothy, pretend you are at this breakfast, and they are serving crepes." In a very sophisticated tone she asked, "Would you say, please pass the syrup (seeer up) or with a countrified drawl, "would you say, please pass the syrup (surr-up)"? Realizing that this was another attempt to belittle her, Dorothy answered, "I'd say, pass the molasses please." After the laughter subsided, Dorothy was sent to the principal's office.

The principal told Dorothy that he had heard the teacher's degrading comments and had already reprimanded her on several occasions. Then he said, "The school year is almost over. She will not be here next year. Go back to class and take comfort in knowing that this will be the last year she will be in a position to embarrass and degrade students at this school, or any other if I have anything to say about it."

True to his word the teacher's contract was not renewed. A few years later the principal became the president of Oklahoma A&M (renamed Oklahoma State University). Dorothy graduated from high school and worked her way through Business College. Her first job after college was secretary for a district judge. Afterwards, she became the secretary for a local businessman. She married the boss and began a family. That proud, defiant, country girl, who would not allow anyone to make her feel insignificant, did all right. During her life time she was on first name terms with senators, governors, a university president, successful businessmen, and many others who were from all stations in life. She treated them all with the same demeanor and respect. I'm proud of her; she was my mother.

CHAPTER 13

Looking for Alice

DURING MY HIGH SCHOOL YEARS I HAD SEVERAL CLOSE FRIENDS. WE were different, yet we had much in common. All made good grades in school and attended church regularly. The boys played football, and the girls were in pep squad or band. No one in the group drank alcohol, and we thought a drug problem was failure of the pharmacist to fill your prescription in a timely manner. By today's standards we might have seemed dull and unexciting. This was far from the truth.

One friend, Joe, was fun to be with but you never knew what to expect. He had a mischievous nature that set him apart from all the others. Joe and I traveled to Oklahoma City to purchase parts for his hot rod. Having completed our shopping, we were walking toward my car when Joe saw what he described as, "The most beautiful girl I have ever seen". He had used that phrase to describe many girls in the past, but this time I had to agree. She was about our age, had long brown hair, and dressed in the latest teenage fashion. She had a nice figure and a pleasant smile. Joe sprang into action as if in a hypnotic trance. She was standing on a corner with her back toward us waiting for the traffic light to change. Joe walked up to her calling out the name, "Alice". Moving around her he hugged her and planted a kiss that would have made Clark Gable jealous. Pulling away he said in a very disturbed voice, "You're not Alice! You're not Alice!"

She said, "I know I'm not Alice!"

He replied, "My name is Joe. What's your name?" In an apologetic tone, she said her name was Betty.

"Betty, I want you to meet John, he's a good friend of mine." He motioned me over and introduced us. After the introduction Joe continued, "John sure thought you were Alice. We're in town to buy auto parts. Right now we're looking for a good restaurant to have lunch. Do you know of a place near that you would recommend?"

She gave us directions to a lunch counter in the next block. Joe invited her to be our guest which she surprisingly accepted. During lunch Betty inquired about Alice.

Joe told her that he and Alice had been childhood sweethearts. She had move to Oklahoma City three years ago and he did not know her Address. He wanted to contact her but was unable to find her. It made a very romantic story. By the time we had finished lunch, Joe had arranged for a date the next time he was in town. If I had attempted Joe's approach, a slap across the face would have been my reward, but he started a new romance. Things seem to always work out great for Joe. He also out-fumbled me for the check.

CHAPTER 14

Big Target

J. T. WAS AT HIS OFFICE WHEN HIS WIFE CALLED, "YOU'RE GOING TO have to talk with the boys when you get home tonight."

"What's the trouble?" J. T. asked.

"It's too long a story to tell you over the phone. I'll tell you when you get home."

J.T. could not stand the suspense and left the office early that evening.

"What kind of trouble have the boys gotten into, Dorothy?"

Dorothy asked him to sit down and not look at her or comment while she told the story. She was afraid if he looked at her she might begin laughing and would not be able to continue.

"You know that your oldest son is in the sixth grade and has discovered girls. He thinks he is madly in love with Pat Miner. Joel and Pat were walking home from school today. Johnny was ahead of them and for some reason Pat began to call him 'fatty'. Johnny was a half a block ahead of them, but could hear her clearly. He was not going to let that go without some kind of come back. He said, 'I had rather be fat than have a mouth so big that I could hit it with a clod of dirt from a half a block away.' Pat thought that was funny. She threw her head back and began to laugh. Johnny picked up a small sand rock and let it fly. Believe it or not, it hit her right in the mouth!!

Joel, of course, had to protect the love of his life and took out after Johnny. With a half a block head start, Johnny reached the front door first and immediately came to me for protection. I got them settled down and told them you would be talking to them tonight. Joel went over to Pat's house to see if she was ok. She was not hurt, but Joel said, 'She sure did a lot of spitting'. Now, what are you going to do?"

Dorothy was right when she looked at J.T. He was trying his best to keep from laughing. As their eyes met, there was an outburst of uncontrollable laughter.

After a few minutes J.T. said,

"I don't know what Pat is going to have for supper tonight, but I bet it's gritty." This comment did not help in getting to a serious discussion about the corrective actions to be taken. He did manage to say, "I'll talk to them."

That night J.T. gathered the boys for a serious discussion. He told Johnny that he must not throw rocks at anybody, and he must apologize to Pat the following day. Joel was to look out for his brother regardless of who was picking on him, and that would include his girl friend. "How would you like to be called names?" Joel said he was sorry, and things seemed to be settled.

The next day J.T. questioned Johnny about the apology to Pat. "Did you do what I told you, Johnny?"

"Yes, I did, Daddy."

"What did you say?"

"I told her I wanted to apologize and I said I was sorry that her mouth was so big that I could hit it with a clod of dirt from half a block away. Is that ok?"

"Oooh! Yes, but don't apologize again, son."

CHAPTER 15

Opportunity Lost

THE TICKER TAPE MACHINE AT THE HUGO DAILY HAD BEEN OPERATING at its normal pace. While I waited for my news papers, I enjoyed listing to the sound of the ticker tape printing news from all parts of the world. It was exciting to think of the people who were gathering and forwarding the information. All that work and effort to keep the folks in Hugo knowledgeable of current events was amazing to me. The machine would print a story, sit idle for a few moments, and begin anew.

Ordinarily, by this time of day I would have been half way through my paper route but for some reason, unknown to me, the work was running behind schedule. Perhaps a reporter had an important story, or maybe it was due to equipment trouble. It was not for me, a sixth grade school boy, to question when the day's edition hit the street. If the papers were delivered an hour later than usual, it would be all right. The news would remain the same.

All of a sudden the ticker tape took off. Print was coming from the machine like I had never seen before. It didn't stop and start again as usual. I could tell it was something important. I looked at the print and could hardly believe my eyes. I called one of the reporters,

"Come look at this message. I'm not sure, but I think you need to see this."

The reporter reluctantly came to the machine, griping under his breath about not having time for such a trivial task. I showed him the story in question. He immediately threw up his hands and ran outside the building shouting. All the people inside the stores and along the street began to take up his call. Drivers got out of their cars and left them setting in the middle of the street. What a celebration!!!

In the meantime, I stood alone in front of the ticker tape machine with my mouth open.

"Could this be the only time in my life that I will have an opportunity to announce such sensational news?"

Talk about a front page type reset! The paper was definitely late that day. Everyone wanted a copy. Not for any news, they already were aware of everything that was on the front page. They just wanted to see it in print. That would make it official.

As the days passed, I heard the reporter relate how he had first read the news and how excited he was. Telling how he ran up and down the streets spreading the news and how various people reacted. It made a great story at Don's Café. The coffee drinkers would hang onto every word. Not once did I hear him mention how his attention was drawn to the news flash. Talk about reporters not revealing their source! That was ok, because I knew I was the first person in Hugo to know, "World War II was over".

CHAPTER 16

Paint Chips

I WAS VISITING AT JOE'S HOUSE WHEN HIS MOTHER ANNOUNCED THAT she was going downtown to buy paint for their living room and kitchen. We had agreed that if she got the materials we would apply the paint. Joe told her,

"They have used paint on sale at the hardware store."

She seemed pleased and replied, "I'm always looking for a bargain."

While waiting for her return, my friend and I began working on his car. When she returned, we cleaned our hands and made our way from the garage to the house. His mother, who was normally a calm person, was standing just inside the door. As Joe stepped into the house, she hit him across the backside with a broom.

She explained, "I went to the hardware store and asked to see the used paint you said was on sale. The clerk asked me to repeat what I said, and I did. He said, 'I'm sure your son was just kidding. Think about what you're saying.' I felt like a fool. I was so embarrassed I left the store immediately. I know word of my request for used paint will be all over town before the sun sets."

His mother seemed to be willing to let the subject go, but Joe made the mistake of laughing. After which he headed for my car with his mother behind him swinging that broom like a major leaguer. I was not far behind him, and we drove away leaving his mother standing in the driveway with the broom on her shoulder.

At first Joe wanted to spend the night at my house, but after an hour he decided that it would probably be safe to go home.

She apologized the next day. She admitted she was mad at herself but had taken her frustrations out on Joe. If he just hadn't laughed, things might have been different. We painted the living room and kitchen three weeks later, and no mention was made about the used paint episode.

CHAPTER 17

Peach Tree Discipline

As a young boy, there were times when it was necessary for my parents to correct my behavior. This parental duty was shared by mother and dad. I seldom took my mother's attempts to discipline seriously, unless she called me by my full name. Otherwise, I knew if I could get her to laugh, the punishment would not be severe. One day my brother and I were misbehaving. After mother had exhausted the usual attempts to corral our actions, she announced that she was calling the police.

Our telephone was an upright model. It had a cradle-shaped support extending from the side of the phone on which the ear piece would normally hang when not in use. The phone would operate only when the ear piece was off the support. She picked up the telephone and asked the operator to connect her with the police department. She held the ear piece to her ear with her left hand and spoke into the mouth piece which she held in her right hand. Hidden from us was her index finger holding down the ear piece support. My brother and I were transfixed on her and wondered what she might say to the police. She had never taken such drastic actions before.

Right in the middle of her pretend conversation the phone rang! She screamed and threw the phone half way across the room. By the time my brother and I quit rolling on the floor laughing, the entire misbehaving incident was forgotten.

Poor mother, she tried so hard to raise her two sons to be polite gentlemen. When she became desperate, she did have a fall back position, "I'll tell your father when he gets home." That was the kiss of death. From that moment we were as good as could be in hopes that mother would have a change of heart or possibly even forget to tell dad. This sometimes worked, but not always. Waiting for dad to come home was pure torture.

After supper dad would say, "Son, we better go to the barn." He would repeat what mother had told him and ask for my response. Of course, mother had given an accurate description of the incident in question, and there was little to say except to express sorrow for my actions. After discussing the situation a bit, Dad would ask what I thought would be fair punishment. This was always the worst part. I would have to sentence myself! Generally, I stated that a whipping was warranted. Dad did not always agree. Sometimes I was required to apologize to mother and anyone who might have witnessed my misbehavior. If a whipping was necessary, I had to select a switch from the peach tree behind the barn. I hated that tree and wished that it might some how become diseased and die. As far as I know, that peach tree is still there producing switches. I never felt mistreated when I was punished, and I was aware that the punishment was fair and deserving.

CHAPTER 18

Got My Ticket

Bob was late stopping at Don's café for coffee this morning. He had been involved working a traffic accident which threw him behind his regular schedule.

"I'll have a donut with my coffee this morning."

Don said, "Chief, you have a good group of people in your force. I really like Hank. He's very friendly and polite even while enforcing the laws. He gave me a ticket for running a stop sign yesterday, and he was so nice I almost thanked him before it was over. I just thought you would want to know what a good man you have on the job."

Bob thanked him and said, "Hank told me about it and was wondering if he could still come in for coffee."

"Sure can. I would miss him if he quit coming and the waitresses would really be upset. He's quite a ladies' man isn't he?"

As Bob mulled over Don's comment about Hank being a ladies man he recalled the infamous ski trip. Hank had signed up for a ski trip to Colorado. The week before the trip was scheduled; he changed his mind and asked for time off to cancel his reservation and get his deposit. When he arrived at the travel agency, the owner saw him come through the door and greeted him with,

"I've been trying to get in touch with you. The ski trip you signed up for is women only, and I'll have to give you your money back. You can schedule another trip at a later date."

Hank thought a minute and replied, "I signed up for this trip in good faith. I paid my deposit and have the receipt. I'm going on that trip!!"

Everyone gathered at the agency for the long bus ride to the ski area. There were several beautiful young ladies lined up ready to board the bus. Hank looked over the crowd for the most appealing girl and offered to carry her luggage. He managed to sit beside her and arranged a date to ski together. He told her that he was an excellent skier. Actually this would be only the second time he had been skiing. When they met at the lift, he noticed that she had selected a championship run. Hank recalled later that a large lump came in his throat but he said nothing because she was, "Just so good looking". He would try to think of some manly way to get out of the situation later.

They got on the lift and headed to the top of the mountain. Cautiously moving to the start of the run, he looked down and saw a shear drop off. It was time to tell the truth. As he twisted his body around to confess his lack of skiing skills, he went over the edge. Witnesses said he was upright for the first two hundred yards or so. The fall broke his leg in several places. Hank was in a cast for six months.

"Yes, Don, you're right. He's a ladies' man. I've known him to go head-over-heels about a woman."

CHAPTER 19

Special Delivery

Several of Dr. John's friends were having coffee and conversation at Don's cafe when he arrived. The topic under discussion was T.W. Lambert, the town miser. Each person told of his experience with T. W. and how he had managed to get the best of them during their various business dealings. When one completed his story, the others would laugh and indicate, "I can top that." They ranked each story by first, second, and third place based on who had been the most foolish and/or gullible. It was agreed that Gary Wallace was number one and was likely to stay in that position a long time. Dr. John listened intently and was amused by their tales of woe.

Gary asked, "Doc, have you had any dealings with T.W.?"

He told them that he knew T.W. when he saw him but had no contact other

than a casual greeting. They warned him that if he should have any business dealings to be very careful.

"He will never out-best me after hearing your problems. No, you can rest assured, I'll be extremely cautious," Doc replied with an air of confidence.

Several months later T. W. entered the doctor's office early one morning. He told the doctor that his wife was very sick and was wondering if he could make a house call. The doctor asked what her symptoms were.

T. W. replied, "She's complaining about stomach cramps. She seems to be in real pain. What do you charge for a house call?"

"My charge will be $15.00." said Dr. John. This was $5.00 more than he normally charged but considering whom he was dealing with, the doctor wanted to be on the safe side. Also, he thought it would be only right for someone in town to get the better of this character.

"I'll pay you now. You will leave right away, won't you?" Dr. John assured him he would leave immediately.

T.W. gave him $15.00 and said, "I'll need a receipt marked paid in full for my records. If you put on there what it's for, that would be helpful."

The doctor thought, "That is a good idea. I want a full record when dealing with this person. He remembered the warning he had received."

Dr. John handed T.W. the receipt, "You can see it's marked, 'Paid in Full. To attend to Mrs. Lambert—Symptoms stomach cramps'."

On the way to Lambert's house the doctor was very proud of the way he had handled T.W. He just realized that his initials probably stood for "tight wad" and wondered if any of his friends had made that connection. He would ask later in the day. If not, he would surely receive their praises for having thought of it. He was certain they would be pleased about the extra $5.00 charge for a house call.

When Dr. John arrived at the Lambert house, a neighbor lady met him at the door. "Thank goodness you're here, Doctor. She's in terrible pain."

When he entered the bedroom where Mrs. Lambert was located, he realized her "stomach cramps" were about to give birth. He spent the better part of the day delivering a six pound boy. Several times he thought of the carefully worded receipt. "Paid in Full. To attend Mrs. Lambert." He had spent all day delivering a baby for $15.00.

The Lambert boy was about one year old before Doc could tell his story at Don's Café. From that time forward his friends addressed him as, "Doc, number one."

CHAPTER 20

That's Bull

All youngsters aspire to do great things with their lives. When I was very young, I wanted to be a fireman, a policeman, a soldier, and a fighter pilot, to name a few. I could see myself in each of these situations. In my fantasies I was always a hero. I arrested the FBI's most wanted, saved a beautiful girl from a burning building, and shot down enemy planes. My most unusual notion was to be a hot tamale salesman. There was a man who pushed a cart around Hugo selling hot tamales. He always made people laugh and seemed to be very happy in his work. I gave that up quickly because I couldn't imagine doing anything heroic or extraordinary selling tamales.

As I grew older, the reality of my limitations and opportunities became clear. It was not disappointing to realize that I would probably never accomplish all those wonderful things I had imagined. It was similar to the time I found out about Santa Claus. That was just the way things were. I no longer had a desire to save the world. That would have to wait, at least, until I had graduated from high school. My attention was turned to school, football, baseball, track, and girls.

However, there was one incident that occurred when I was a sophomore that took me back to my Walter Mitty fantasies. The land around Hugo was good cattle country. Several families made their living raising horses and cattle. Because of the interest created by that industry, there were rodeo contests in Hugo and other towns in the surrounding area. There was to be a rodeo sponsored by the Future Farmers of America (FFA), at Antlers Oklahoma. The contest was open to high school students only. I thought this could be the first step to a national all-around cowboy championship award. There were several events that one could enter. I considered all options and decided on bull riding. Bulls were not as high off the ground as horses, and that would be to my advantage. With entry papers completed, all was ready except for the proper dress. I had Levi blue jeans and a shirt, but no Stetson hat or boots. A trip to the People's Department Store, and my wardrobe was complete.

As the day of the rodeo approached, I was beginning to have second thoughts about participating. The only comfort I had was the idea that since this was for high school kids the animals would be sized accordingly. That was reassuring to me. When we received word of the animal we had drawn to ride, several of the guys who were familiar with the stock told me, "You've lucked out and drawn Tornado, the meanest, largest, and most notorious bull in the lot. You will get a good score riding him." I suppose they thought this made me happy. Well, they were wrong!

There was a great deal of excitement around the loading pen where the bulls were being transferred from a stockade to the riding chutes. Men's heads were popping up above the fencing like a jack-in-the-box. Each time this bull collided with the fence the vibrations could be felt several feet away. As the bull came into view, I knew why men were climbing the fence to get away from the monster. That was the biggest, meanest-looking bull I had ever seen. He was solid black, his nostrils were flared, and he had a wild look in his eyes. He was pawing dirt, throwing it in the air with his front feet.

"Boy! I'm glad I don't have to get near that thing. I pity the poor sucker that gets him."

My stomach turned over several times when I heard a handler call him Tornado. One of the men yelled a few names that I won't repeat and kicked him on the rump.

"Don't kick him! He's mad enough now!" I hollered

When it came time for me to ride, I got over the beast, fitted my grip in the halter and waited the announcement for my entrance. About the same time the announcer said, "Out of gate 2 is Johnny Wall riding Tornado", the bull moved and I got off. This occurred three times. "For the third time, Johnny Wall from gate number 2 riding Tornado" the announcer repeated. When I attempted to get off again, my brother pushed me down and yelled,

"Open the gate."

As the bull exited the chute, he rubbed his side along the gate post catching my leg and pushed me back to his rear end. There I was, out in the arena, sitting on the rear end of that bull with my left arm fully extended holding on and waving my right arm in the air. Some people thought I was waving my arm trying to keep my balance, but I was really signaling for help. I bounced from the tail to the head and back again several times. I didn't know if I was more scared to stay on or to be thrown off. I sure didn't want to be in the same arena with that bull loose. Before I knew it, the ride was over, and I was flat on my back lying on the ground. Several guys in clown suits distracted the bull while someone helped me up.

"That was a great ride. You'll get to ride again tonight," someone said. That was not what I wanted to hear.

I asked him how he knew that, and he answered,

"Didn't you hear the whistle?"

"No, I heard someone screaming. I think it was me!" I replied.

I was instructed to see what time I should report for the evening event and find out which bull I would be riding.

"No thanks, I've got other plans for tonight."

I knew holding my girlfriend's hand at a movie would be better than holding on to another bull. On the way home I tried to remember my thoughts between the times that gate opened and when I hit the ground, but couldn't recall. One thing was certain; I knew my claim to fame, if any, would not be on the back of something hairy, with horns.

CHAPTER 21

That's My Hook

The clock on the wall at Wright's Auto Parts read 5:00 PM. Jim Cornett was already headed toward the front door when the second hand reached twelve. He had worked afternoons at the auto supply store since football season was over, and he was ready for a break. It was the first week of summer vacation from high school. Jim and his friends were taking their annual camping trip. Chuck Stewart and Scooter McGuire had left early that morning to prepare the camp site. Jim and Hugh Tyler wouldn't leave until their work day was completed. That evening Hugh jumped into Jim's car and yelled,

"Four days of fishing, swimming, and goofing off! Let's be off, my good man."

Sure enough, when Jim and Hugh reached the site, the tents were erected, drainage ditches dug, and the camp fire was blazing. After unpacking their gear and food supplies, they sat down to get an update on their friends' activities from earlier in the day.

"We got here about nine o'clock this morning and set up camp. We put the boat in the water and rowed around the lake for a little while. We did some swimming and a little fishing. Didn't have any luck fishing though. Thought you guys might run the trotline. Fish would sure taste good for supper," Chuck reported.

Scooter started to question the statement about "the trotline" but was immediately interrupted.

"Yes, sir, I bet there are several good fish on there by now! I think I can tell you where we located the trotline. You should be able to find it even though it's dark. Why don't you guys go see? In the meantime Scooter and I will get the rest of the food prepared," Chuck continued.

Jim and Hugh grabbed their flashlights and headed for the boat. Much to their amazement they were able to find the trotline with very little difficulty.

"You get in front of the boat, raise the line and I will hold the light. If we get a fish, you take it off and I'll re-bait the hook." Jim instructed.

They had collected several fish when a voice came out of the darkness.

"What are you guys doing running my trotline?" Jim and Hugh were startled and strained their eyes to see beyond the light flashing in their faces. They could just make out a large man holding what appeared to be a gun.

"This is our trotline! Our friends put it out this afternoon." Jim managed to get the words out although his voice trembled.

Back at the camp site Scooter and Chuck were discussing the trotline situation. Scooter said, "You shouldn't have told them we set that trotline. You could have told them the truth—we found it this afternoon while rowing around the lake. What if they get caught? That's almost as bad as stealing a guy's horse. On the other hand, fish would taste mighty good no matter where they come from."

"I didn't tell them we set the trotline! It's true I may have implied that, but if you recall, I said 'we located' it. If they made the assumption we put it out, it isn't my fault." Chuck said with a grin.

After a few laughs they forgot about the trotline ownership, and began to peal potatoes for supper.

"There's nothing that tastes better than fried potatoes with fish. What do you think we should do to start the day off in the morning?" Chuck commented. They continued to make plans for the following day when they heard the sound of gunfire.

Scooter said, "That sounded like two shots from a shotgun. Of course it could be one shot and we heard an echo. What do you think?"

"Don't know. There could have been two shots. It's hard to tell how many or where it's coming from" Chuck replied. "If we go swimming first thing in the morning, breakfast would taste better. Having a good appetite improves our cooking considerably."

"I agree, particularly if Jim cooks. I wonder where they are. They should have been back several minutes ago. Do you think anything's wrong? I'm worried. You shouldn't have told them we set that line."

Scooter replied. "You don't think I would deliberately try to deceive them?" There was a sound of something moving through the brush. "There they come now. Don't worry. They know how to take care of themselves." declared Chuck.

Suddenly there appeared a large man standing at the edge of the camp site. In the dim light of the campfire the stranger looked seven feet tall. "I'll teach you guys to run someone's trotline!" A blast from a shotgun pierced the night air!

It would be difficult to say which boy threw his potato the highest. One thing was for sure—they would not be around when the potatoes hit the ground. They ran through the brush and into the darkness with the speed of a great running back.

They ran for approximately five minutes before they stopped to see if anyone was following.

Scooter struggled to listen. "Don't hear anyone."

"Thank goodness! I've gone about as far as I can through these thorns and low-hanging limbs. Look at me. My cloths are torn to pieces along with me in them," Chuck moaned.

Scooter replied, "At least you didn't fall in a ditch full of mud. How are we going to get back to the car? We have to report this to the sheriff. What are we going to say about Jim and Hugh? I can just see them floating face down in that lake! Do you suppose they're all right?"

"I don't think so. That guy is crazy. There's no telling what he did. I wish I had never mentioned that trotline. We'll work ourselves up to the clearing at the camp site and watch for our chance to run for the car. Here are the keys; you're faster than I am. How quick can you get it started?"

"Darn fast if I'm looking down the barrel of a shotgun!!!" Scooter answered.

After waiting several minutes, they slowly retraced their path back toward the camp site. Would the 'crazy' still be there? Can we get to the car without him seeing us? These were the thoughts going through their minds as they neared the camp site.

The aroma of fried potatoes was detected as they came closer. Ordinarily that smell would have tempted their taste buds, but right now eating was the last thing on their agenda.

"He's fixing our potatoes!" Chuck whispered.

At the clearing they carefully pushed aside the branches in order to get a clear view of the camp. Much to their surprise seated around the fire enjoying fried fish and potatoes was Jim, Hugh, and Paul Neilson, the sports writer for the Hugo Daily.

As Chuck and Scooter stepped into the clearing, Jim said,

"Where have you guys been? Come and get some food. As you know, nothing tastes better with fish than fried potatoes. You look terrible."

Paul added with a grin, "Why did you run when we shot in the air? We were just letting you know we were back. You don't think we would deliberately try to deceive you into thinking we were shooting at you, do you?"

CHAPTER 22

The One That Didn't Get Away

There were three topics of conversation at Don's Café that always created a lot of participation: Hugo High football, politics, and fishing. Of course there would be other things discussed like new car models, or weather, etc. However, the more boisterous sessions were about the aforementioned topics. Football and politics were seasonal, but fishing could be bantered about year round. Several of the regulars who had coffee at Don's Café were fisherman. There were different opinions as to who was the best fisherman, but one name that was always included in the top three was Charles Bass Simons. He made an art of fishing, and when he talked, everyone listened. They never knew when he might reveal a secret on technique or equipment. Most fishermen share some of their knowledge, but like a good cook they don't tell the entire recipe. His reputation extended beyond Hugo since he held the record for reeling in the largest bass caught in the state.

Everyone enjoyed hearing him tell the story of his big catch. An article with his picture was not only printed in the local news paper but had state-wide distribution.

Bass always had the latest in fishing tackle. If a better gadget, rod, or reel came on the market, it would not be long before it was in his possession. After WWII fishing boats constructed of aluminum material were available. Prior to the end of the war all aluminum materials and manufacturing were geared toward the war effort. The aluminum boats were much lighter and easier to maneuver than the old wooden boats that everyone had used in the past. Also, outboard motors were beginning to trickle into sporting goods shops for sale to the public. No one was surprised that Bass Simons was the first person in Hugo to own a new aluminum boat and a seven and one half horsepower outboard motor.

Hugo was surrounded by three rivers and several beautiful lakes, all of which were considered to be "good fishing holes". Bass owned a small cabin on Schooler Lake, and it was his favorite place to spend time trying new fishing techniques. He enjoyed going fishing early in the mornings and coming in for a nice breakfast of coffee, bacon, and eggs around eight o'clock.

On this morning he would try the aluminum boat for the first time. After a few hours of fishing it was nearing eight o'clock and time for breakfast. Crossing the main body of the lake, he opened the motor wide. He thought, "This must make an impressive picture passing over the water at such a high speed". Halfway across the lake he spotted a large log floating half submerged. There had been several heavy rains recently, and the log had been set adrift by high winds and rising water. Bass immediately recognized the danger and decided to tow the log to shore. He attached a rope to the log and began to move toward the boat dock. As he neared the area of the boat dock, he noticed several of his coffee drinking friends on shore waving.

"They've come to see my boat. I'll speed up and give them a show", he thought.

The strain of several pounds drag created by the log would not be easily overcome. Slowly the boat began to pick up speed.

"Looks like you caught a big one," someone hollered, referring to the log. Bass could not hear what they were saying over the sound of the motor but smiled and waved.

"I'll be in shortly and give you a ride in my boat," Bass replied. Minutes later he had the boat lined up ready to dock. He was anxious for his friends to try their hand at guiding the boat around the lake. To illustrate his boat handling prowess he would approach the dock at full throttle. At just the right time he would swing the motor around to reverse and make a perfect landing.

The next series of events occurred so rapidly that they can only be described in slow motion. Had a movie camera been available, the results would have been a classic tutoring device for young actors. All emotions known to man would be illustrated, frame by frame, through Bass's facial expressions.

Frame one: Friendship, joy, and pride. As Bass made the perfect docking, he displayed a big smile indicating joy seeing his friends, and there was just a hint of pride in having accomplished something well.

Frame two: Confused and bewildered. "Why are they waving and pointing? What are they trying to tell me? This motor makes too much noise."

Frame three: Horror and fear. "Now, the motor is off. What are they saying? The log!!! The Log!!! I forgot about the log!!! It's headed straight for the boat!!!!!"

Frame four: Embarrassment, anger, humility, humor: As the log collided with the boat, water began to fill the vessel. Slowly the boat sank with Bass going down with his ship like a true captain. Luckily the depth of the lake at that location was three feet.

"How stupid can I be? Right in front of everybody!! This makes me so mad.... but if I show anger, they will never let me forget this."

With that thought in mind Bass announced that he wanted to show his latest catch. Hugging the log, which was now floating directly over his boat, he said,

"Isn't this a beauty?"

There was a picture in the local paper with Bass standing in waste deep water hugging his log. The caption read, "LOCAL FISHERMAN BAGS ANOTHER RECORD. (Not seen in photo is his new aluminum boat in which Mr. Simons is standing. Details on page four)."

CHAPTER 23

The Things Boys Do

THE COUNTRY HAD SUFFERED THROUGH A DEEP ECONOMIC DEPRESSION during the thirties. On December 7, 1941, we entered World War II. As a result of these two events, most people in town had few material goods. There was rationing during the war. Items such as coffee, gasoline, meat, rubber products, bubble gum, and sugar were on the list of things in limited supply. In spite of the shortcomings, growing up in Hugo during the thirties and forties was a wonderful time.

During the war there were drives sponsored by the civic leaders to gather scrap metal, foil, rubber and paper. The person who gathered the most would receive a savings bond. These drives were exciting and kept all the kids busy searching, hoping to find enough material to finish in first place. It was not so much for the savings bond that we worked hard, but rather the thrill of winning. The competition was intense.

When we were not involved in some civic project, it was time for play. We had great fun when all the neighborhood boys got together to play. The fact we had little afforded us the opportunity to use our imagination. Much of our time was spent playing "war". A branch from a tree could be a machine gun. A cardboard box made a fine armored tank or a B-17 bomber. We never lost a battle nor suffered any casualties. We longed to get in the real action!!

There were unsung heroes arising from every activity we undertook. No one bragged about his accomplishments. There was no need. The proof was in the doing. For instance Tommy could throw a ball further than anyone. Billy was best at horseback riding and sling shot. Hugh got more hits in our ball games. I lifted the most weights, and my brother could burp louder than anyone.

The outcome of our games was predictable. Billy would win the horse race. Tommy would throw the winning touchdown pass. Hugh would drive the winning run home in our softball games. Yes, everything was generally predictable except for one winter activity—Pee writing in the snow.

The contest would be scheduled following the first heavy snow storm every year. Of course there were rules which were strictly enforced.

1. The snow had to be 4 inches deep or greater.
2. Had to spell your name or nick name.
3 Name must contain at least 4 letters.
4. Letter "I" must be dotted and "T" crossed.
5. Print or longhand writing accepted.
6. Wind less than 5 miles per hour.
7. Extra points awarded for printing (stop and go action required).

This contest was always in doubt. It was rare that the same person would win twice in a row. On occasion someone would attempt to print for extra points but was never successful. I'm certain this activity was where we learned to write in longhand.

As we grew older our activities as a neighborhood group dwindled. We still played ball and other games, but for organized team play at school. All of us excelled in one or more sport. Tommy threw the pass that won the district championship in high school football. Bill played the tuba in the marching band. Some worked during the summers to earn a few dollars for spending money. We were beginning to notice girls, and that required funds for cokes, movies, and gifts for special occasions.

The war in which we wanted to participate passed us by. The conflict in Korea didn't. There was at least one of the neighborhood crew in every branch of the service. We joked and said, "That's why we won." Although we have gone our separate ways, we still remain friends and visit often. Remembering back to the good old days, we sometimes greet one another, "How's your peemanship?"

The Neighborhood Boys

CHAPTER 24

Corn Silk

Sometimes growing up can seem terribly slow. The signs of adulthood need a push occasionally. When I was around ten years old a situation arose that required immediate action. My older brother, Bill, and I would go skinny dipping in the pond on our farm. Naturally we would compare our attributes. One difference that stood out immediately was the hair on my brother's body. He was very proud and mentioned it at every opportunity, just in case we had not noticed. This went on for several days. Bill and I had our fill of his bragging. But what were we to do? Only time could change the situation.

Maybe not! Bill and I decided that corn silk placed in the appropriate places on our bodies would serve as a means of competing in the race for manhood. We gathered a large amount of hair-like fiber (corn silk) from several ears of corn. We stored the fiber and glue in a safe place near the pond in preparation for our next swimming venture.

Our grand entrance to the pool was met with surprise, shock, and laughter. My brother thought we were crazy. We had more hair than a full grown gorilla. As we swam, the water based glue gave way to the truth. Corn silk was floating everywhere. Our disguise was a failure.

However, it did stop his bragging. I guess he was afraid of what we would try next.

We have had many laughs about our antics through the years. It's a good thing super glue had not been invented, or we would still be picking corn silk from our arm pits, chest, and elsewhere.

CHAPTER 25

The Un-Paid Ticket

It was two o'clock and time for my weekly afternoon chemistry lab. This was the most dreaded class of my college experience. A two hour class in the late afternoon, when it seemed that all other students were through for the day, reached the limits of my endurance.

This day I was driving my mother's car since mine was in the shop for repair. Her car didn't have a student decal, and I parked in the two-hour visitors' parking near the chemistry building. As the class began, the professor announced we would have a discussion about the experiment after everyone had finished. Each completed his work in record time, except two students. They had been late for class and were several minutes behind. I didn't think it was right for the entire class to wait until they were through. It was obvious we would be running beyond the time for class to dismiss. But I was not in charge and could do nothing but sit and wait with twenty one other disgusted students. Finally, we were allowed to leave. Twenty minutes of our free time had been wasted.

When I arrived at mother's car, there was a parking ticket prominently displayed beneath the windshield wiper.

"Great, this is what I get because those two knuckleheads were late." I muttered to myself. "This time of day there's not three cars in this whole parking lot. It's not like I was taking up a space someone needed. I think I will put this ticket where it belongs—in the trash can."

Having disposed of the undeserved citation, I drove home not giving the incident another thought. Several weeks had passed when I received notice from the campus police to come in and pay the overdue parking ticket fine. They had tracked me down through my mother's car license tag. I threw the letter in the trash.

"That's mother's car, what can they do to me?" I thought. As time passed I received several notices which I immediately dispatched to the waste receptacle. The fine had increased with each notice and was up to $3.00 when I received word that I had been suspended from school. I was not to attend classes in the future until this matter was settled.

It occurred to me these guys were serious. It would be a matter of wills from this point on. It was not about money, I could handle that, but it was a matter of principle. Would I give up my belief that the ticket was undeserved and pay the fine? It was time to have a face-to-face confrontation.

When I walked into the campus police station, I showed the last letter I had received to the man at the desk. "Oh, yes. We expected you would be dropping in anytime." I could tell from the smirk on his face he was very familiar with my case. He opened the cash draw and said, "That will be three dollars cash or check." He seemed very sure of himself. "Not so fast", I thought. He hasn't heard my story which I proceeded to tell,

"That was not my car but belongs to my mother. I'm not responsible for her parking when on campus." This would clear everything up and I didn't exactly lie. If he wants to assume that my mother parked the car, well, that is his choice. I felt very good about the whole situation.

The desk sergeant began, "If you had read the rules set down when you got your student parking decal, you would have found that you are responsible for your parents' parking while on campus. Now will that be cash or check?"

He seemed proud of himself. He's quoting rules to me!! He's got me. My shoulders slumped. I had been defeated. Then a thought entered my numbed brain.

"Well, I have a brother enrolled in school here and I want him expelled today! He is as much responsible as I am."

A look of bewilderment and shock replaced the smirk on the desk sergeant's face. He was quiet for a few seconds. At that instant I knew I had him. He tore the ticket up and instructed me to leave. As I went out the door, he said,

"And tell your mother never to park on this campus again!"

Later that day I told my brother what happened. For some unknown reason he became excited. "You said what!!!" he exclaimed. I told him "I would never have let things go so far as to have you kicked out of class. After all, what are brothers for if not to look out for one another?"

Many years have passed since my brother and I graduated from that university. My mailing address has changed several times. But still, when I go through the daily mail I expect to see an old beat-up letter, which has been forwarded many times, telling me: Do not go to classes until the $10,000.00 overdue parking fine has been settled.

CHAPTER 26

Tough Times

Folks in Washington D.C. were calling it a depression. Those who worked for a living called it "tough times". Regardless of what you call it, several Hugo citizens were having great difficulties making ends meet. Jim Sanders thought it was time for action. He spoke to Gary Wallace about providing a helping hand to those in need.

"That's a great idea! We could ask Chief Baker and Coach Parker to meet and form a plan," Gary suggested.

"Why limit it to a few? It's everyone's duty to help a neighbor. Let's have a town meeting and enlist everyone. You know most will join and be glad to do so," Jim answered.

"You bet! There're good people in this town. Hold it!!! I see a problem with that idea. If we have a town meeting, T.W. will be there, and you know how outspoken he is. He's against everything. The old grouch! He'll ruin the whole idea. Before it's over, he will have everyone upset and have the town divided. Half the people will be ready to throw rocks at him, and the other half will be aiming at us!" Gary exclaimed.

"You let me worry about T. W. Get a meeting scheduled for next Tuesday night at seven o'clock. I'll act as moderator. Talk to Schooler about an article in the paper and get a few spots on the radio. I'm going to be out of town, but I'll be back for the meeting. Don't tell anyone, and I mean anyone, what the meeting is about."

The American Legion Hall was filling up. It was large enough to hold several hundred, and a stage from which to address the crowd. Although Coach Parker and Chief Baker didn't know the reason for meeting, they had agreed to sit on the stage with Gary and Jim to show their support.

"Turnout is going to be good. I see T.W. has taken a seat on the front row. That figures," Gary said as he surveyed the audience.

"It's time to get started. Where the heck is Jim? I thought he was supposed to be the moderator," Chief Baker inquired.

"He was out of town day before yesterday, but he said he would be back in plenty of time to make this meeting. It was his idea in the first place. I can't believe he would be late. Let's take our place on stage. Hopefully he will show up by the time we get settled. If he doesn't show, I guess I'll say something first and call on you guys to comment on Jim's proposal. Ok?" Gary said reluctantly. Gary was thanking the people for coming and explaining about the moderator being detained when Jim appeared at the backstage door. His hair was uncombed, pants wrinkled, and shirt tail partially out.

"Well, folks, I spoke too soon. Here's your moderator right now. I'll turn the microphone over to someone you all know, Jim Sanders." Gary whispered, "Thank goodness," under his breath as he was seated.

"Sorry I'm late, folks. I've had problems like you wouldn't believe."

T.W. hollered out, "We believe it. You look like the tail end of destruction. What have you been up to? No good I suspect."

"I know I don't look like much. Thanks for bringing that to everyone's attention." This comment drew a few laughs from the crowd as Jim tucked in his shirt and patted down his hair.

"Since you asked about my problem, T.W., I'll explain.

Ya'll know I own timberland near Malvern, Arkansas. I was over there checking on the seedlings I had planted. I just got back late last night. My land is out in the boonies, and I can't find it without asking someone for directions. I stopped at a farm house where a man was standing on his front porch and his little girl, maybe two or three years old, was playing in the front yard. He was getting ready to go to work in his garden and had leaned a hoe against the porch while he tied his shoes.

As we were talking, I looked back in the direction of the road where he was pointing. When I turned to look, I noticed a snake several feet from where the little girl was playing. I told the farmer about the snake. It looked like a brown rattler commonly found in timberland. The man looked over my shoulder and said it would be ok. We continued to talk about the location of my property. Several times I looked back and noticed that the snake was moving closer to the baby. Each time I told that guy he said it would be ok. I couldn't figure out why he didn't take the hoe and kill the snake. After all, the hoe was right there between us. By now the snake was only a few feet from her. It was so close I didn't want to look anymore and turned my back toward the child.

I heard a scream. I jerked around to see what I already knew had happened. We did every thing we could but because of the location of the bite and her size there was not much we could do. By the time we got to the hospital it was too late. To lose a beautiful little baby like that was almost more than I have been able to take. Since then I can't sleep. I've tried to get it off my mind but haven't been able to. I don't know what's wrong with me!!"

The silence in the room was broken by an angry shout from T.W. "I know what's wrong with ya! You feel guilty, and by golly you should. You should've picked up that hoe and killed that snake yourself. I don't give a tinker's dam if that baby's father was there. That doesn't relieve you from responsibility. That baby was in trouble, and you should've helped."

"Do you really feel that way T.W.?" Jim spoke in a surprised but apologetic tone.

"Yeah, I do!"

"Do the rest of you feel like T.W.?" Jim could tell from the lack of response and the fact that no one would look at him, the answer was, "yes".

"Well, I'm glad all of you feel like that. You're exactly right. I should feel guilty. When a person is in need, it is the responsibility of everyone to lend a helping hand. That is what this meeting is about tonight. Although, I made up that story about the little girl and the snake, we have the same situation right here in Hugo! There are people in need. It's time for all of us to do something about it. Turning your back on a problem won't make it go away. I want us to form committees tonight to oversee work parties, coordinate a food bank, employment agent, and any other committee we might see fit to organize."

"Now, we need to select chairman and volunteers for the three committees I mention and, T.W., I would like for you to head up all committees. You would act as a chairman of the chairman. Coordinate their efforts and see to it that everything is working as it should. Will you do it?"

That night the ground work was laid for a very successful endeavor. All the committees were filled. Every person at the meeting volunteered to help. T.W. proved to be the right choice as leader for the program. He was a tough master at arms. If things were not moving fast enough, he would give a gentle nudge and say,

"You've picked up the hoe. Now use it!"

For months he was never seen around town without a smile on his face, something the folks in Hugo had never witnessed before. "Helping people makes me feel good," he would say.

CHAPTER 27

Powder Puffs

Chief of Police Bob Baker's work day generally started with a trip by his office at City Hall to see if anything unusual had occurred during the night. Afterwards, he would drop in at Don's Café to have his morning cup of coffee. Also, he could measure the pulse of the city and catch up on the latest news being discussed by the customers. This morning he was particularly anxious to have coffee since Hugo had won the Friday night football game which clenched the 1948 East District Championship. The Hugo team had been considered a seven point underdog and obviously was not expected to win. He knew the conversation would be exciting to say the least.

The time was nine o'clock and the usual crowd had gathered at Don's Café for coffee and conversation. The café was small with only six booths, two tables near the front window, and ten stools located along a serving counter. Although the space was small, the activity was lively with people drifting in and out to eat and catch up on the latest happenings. This was particularly true on Saturdays following a Friday night high school football game. Every play would be discussed and analyzed with each person contributing his expert opinion as to why a play was or was not successful. The two tables near the window were designated as the official gathering spot for the more serious topics of discussion. Anyone passing could see that a meeting was in session, and they knew all comers were welcome.

As Bob entered the café, Jim Sanders jumped from his chair to give a high five greeting.

"Chief, can you believe those Buffaloes? I'm so proud of those guys.

There was no way they could beat that team except by sheer guts." Jim continued. The remaining crowd agreed, and they began to go over what they felt were the game winning plays. Some of the football players would always come by the café to show their bruises and get the praise and admiration due them. On those rare occasions when the team lost, there were not as many present, but that was understood by all.

This morning most of the team came in two or three at a time for a cup of hot chocolate. After each boy had received much attention he was asked, "How did you fellows manage to come out on top? What did Coach Parker say to you guys?" Almost everyone answered "Coach Parker didn't say anything to us. We were mad! Friday at school each member of the team received a package which was delivered to us by the postman. Delivered right to our classes!!! The package contained a powder-puff with the score written on it Idabel 50 Hugo 0. The postmark was from Idabel so we knew who sent them. If those guys thought we were a bunch of powder-puffs, they don't think it now. We showed them!"

Bob would just smile when they told what had inspired them. He knew who had really sent the packages. Coach Parker had asked him to drive the forty five miles to mail the packages from the Idabel post office. Some day the true story may be told, but it would not come from the Chief of Police. Coach Parker had said more to them than they thought.

Hugo Buffaloes
1948 East district 4A Champs

CHAPTER 28

The Open Door

The year was 1977, and it was my first trip to our nation's capital. This was a business trip, and most of my time would be spent in meetings. There would not be much time for site seeing. My traveling companion, Vic, had been to D.C. several times and said he would act as a guide. We arrived in town before noon, checked into our hotel, then set out for the tour. We visited several monuments and museums. Having completed the tour at the Washington monument, my guide and I realized only one more site visit would be possible. We walked what seemed a mile or more to the Capital Building. It was dusky dark when we arrived. As we approached the building, we could see that there were three doors for possible entry. They were stacked one above the other, and it was obvious they led onto three different levels within the building. We attempted to enter the upper and then the second floor but found the doors locked. We moved down to the basement door, and much to our surprise, the door opened. We traveled down a narrow hall which opened into a large circular room.

By the time Vic and I had reached the center of the room, armed security personnel appeared through two additional hallways on our right and left. The sergeant in charge asked, "How did you get into the building?" We pointed toward the hallway behind us and told him we had entered through the door.

He answered, "Not so, that the door was locked!"

"No, we found it open. We didn't know it was after visiting hours. We realized it was getting late but hoped to make it in time and were pleased to find that we had." I answered.

The sergeant sent one of the guards to look at the door, and he returned to state,

"There was no sign of forcible entry."

We were asked to provide identification and explanation for our visit.

"This is my first visit to D.C. We left Oklahoma City early this morning and arrived around 9:00 o'clock. We have a business meeting in the morning and take a flight back to Oklahoma City at 4:00 tomorrow afternoon. I wanted to see as much as possible." I explained.

He seemed to be satisfied and asked what we wanted to see. I told him that I didn't know since I had never been there before.

"I'll give you a quick tour and then you will have to leave." the sergeant stated as he directed us to one of the hallways. We had a brief thirty or forty minute guided tour. The sergeant would tell interesting stories about certain pieces of furniture or pictures. He spoke of persons who had "lain at state" in the rotunda, as we proceeded through the building.

The end of the tour wound up at the front entry. The sergeant's demeanor changed and he became very serious, animated, and loud.

"This is the front entry to this building. All visitors enter and leave at this door. If you ever return you will use this entry."

Vic and I assured him that we would and thanked him for the tour. As we were walking out the door, he held my arm, leaned over and whispered, "Sorry, I had to do that. They're watching. You guys have a safe trip home. I'm from Muskogee."

CHAPTER 29

Unforgettable

EACH FAMILY HAS AT LEAST ONE MEMBER THAT IS UNIQUE AND unforgettable. In my case it was Aunt Eddie. Actually she was more like a grandmother to me since she had raised my mother. Aunt lived in a small house next door to our home. Dad had built the house for her because mother wanted to look after her as she grew older. For this I will always be grateful. She was dear to me, and I loved her very much.

Aunt was my idea of a true pioneer woman. She was well into her seventies and still planting a vegetable garden every year. I would arrive at her house to find her weeding the garden in ninety degree weather. It did little good to get on to her for working so hard. She had a mind of her own, and if something needed to be done she was going to attempted it. Looking back I'm sure that's what kept her going for eighty seven years.

She had lived during hard times and was very careful with the little money she received from her pension. Aunt looked on the serious side of life. Being very straight laced, she did not approve of "loose living". Playing cards and dance-halls were tools of the devil. She didn't have a sense of humor and did not appreciate a good joke. I was the only one in the family who could joke with her. I teased her quite often and would actually get her to laugh on occasion. Looking at pictures of her when she was young prompted me to ask, "Is it true that you were a dance-hall girl?" Of course I got a resounding "No!" But when I told her she was beautiful and would have been well qualified, she was ok with the question. If anyone else had asked that, she would have swelled up like a toad.

After I left home and was making my own money I would take her out to dinner. She was eager to go and seemed to enjoy herself even though it was just for a short time. I always took her to a nice restaurant and insisted that she order something special. We would have a grand meal and enjoy each other's company. Upon leaving the restaurant she would invariably say, "Thank you, son. A hamburger would have done just as good." This was to let me know she thought I had spent too much on her.

Every time the entire family went out to eat, she would say, "I'll get mine." Aunt knew full well we were not going to let that happen. I picked up her check and was glad to do so. One time mother, Aunt Eddie, my wife, and I were traveling and stopped to get a bite to eat. The waiter made separate tickets for each of us. After we had eaten, I gathered the tickets and started to pay when Aunt said, "I'll get mine." Just for meanness I handed her the ticket. We had traveled several miles and Aunt had not said a word until she asked my wife, "What did you order?" My wife described her order in detail. "How much did it cost?" Aunt inquired. Having heard the cost of my wife's meal she said, "Next time I'm going to get what you did." I nearly ran off the road trying to keep from laughing. When we got her home, I left money for the meal on her kitchen table. As far as I know, the words, "I'll get mine," never passed her lips again as long as she lived. She was a great lady and I'm thankful to have known her.

Youthful Aunt Eddie in her finest

CHAPTER 30

That's My Story

THE TELEPHONE RANG SIX TIMES BEFORE DOROTHY COULD MAKE her way through the piles of clothing, furniture, and knick-knacks she was pricing for a garage sale.

"Why does that phone ring every time I get busy? I sit around here days wanting someone to call and nothing happens. But let me get busy, and the thing rings off the wall. Hello!"

"Dorothy, this is Walter Lanyard. I hope I didn't catch you at a bad time, but something happened this morning I thought you should know. You're going to have to teach Johnny how to use his imagination."

"What has my youngest gotten into this time, Walter?"

"Oh, he's not in trouble. As matter of fact all the teachers, student body, and myself are grateful for his action. Your son and Gene Peters had a difference of opinion. Gene Peters has bullied the kids all year. That is until today. I don't think he will bother anyone from now on."

"For Pete's sake what's happened, Walter?"

"Gene picked on your son during recess this morning and Johnny popped him right in the eye. He'll have a shiner tomorrow. After the blow for freedom was struck, they began to wrestle until one of the teachers broke them up. She mentioned the incident to me. Well, I don't think the teacher intended to make an official report. I believe she was so happy at seeing Gene get what he had coming; she just wanted to share the good news. However, I have a rule that anyone caught fighting will get a whipping."

"Now, Walter, you're the principal. I gave you my permission to discipline the boys when they needed it. I've always told you that," Dorothy restated.

"Not so fast, Dorothy, let me tell you the whole story. I had Gene in my office first to hear his side. According to his story he was totally innocent, and "He had been attacked when he was not looking. Otherwise, Johnny would have never been able to get in a punch." I knew he started the trouble from the teacher's report. So, I gave Gene five good licks with my paddle.

Then I called Johnny to come to the office. I ask him what happened. I've been in the teaching business for thirty plus years and have gone through situations like this many times. His story takes the cake. I didn't want to give him a whipping but rules are rules. Sometimes you have to do things you had rather not do. But after hearing that fantastic story, I knew I could not punish him. It might have stifled his imagination for life, and if he had any more stories like that I sure didn't want to miss them.

Talent to dream a concoction like that needs to be protected. I whacked a pillow in the seat of my chair five times to indicate what might be coming. The noise scared Johnny as much as if I had been hitting him. I think he was measuring the force of the sound and with his vivid imagination could feel each blow. Also, if someone were listening outside, it would have sounded like the real thing. After that, I dismissed him because I just had to laugh. I had been holding it in as long as I could. His story and delivery were so funny. You just had to be there."

"Walter, are you going to tell me what he said or not?

"Oh, didn't I tell you? He said and I quote, 'We were playing and I had my fist doubled up. I fell down, and Gene fell on it.'"

CHAPTER 31

Something In The Air

When the Chief of police Bob Baker left his house this morning, he had no idea that the day's events would include the most talked about unsolved mystery of his law enforcement career. As usual he went by his office to get the over-night activities report

"You guys are doing a good job monitoring the town's activities fromthis office. Now, I'll go see what's really happening in town," Bob said as he laughed and walked out the door. This was interpreted by his office staff as, "I'm going to get coffee at Don's Cafe."

A few minutes later deputy Hank Green stopped by the café to tell Bob that the high school principal had called and requested police immediately.

Hank said. "I don't know what the problem is, but the principal sure was upset."

Bob transferred his freshly-poured coffee into a paper cup and told Hank he had better follow him to school. When Bob entered the school house, he was immediately made aware of the problem. The odor of a skunk was overwhelming.

"Gee whiz! How am I going to locate and trap a skunk?" Bob thought. He had attended Hugo High, and he was aware of all the little nooks and crannies available for an animal to hide.

"I want the person or persons responsible for this to be tracked down and punished. You need to question these three students. I have no idea if they are guilty, but based on the past it's a good place to start your investigation," the principal stated while handing Bob the list of names. Bob was taken to the location where the skunk was found. He was relieved to find that the skunk had already been removed from the building.

Bob interviewed several students but made little progress. He reported his findings to the principle,

"I haven't seen so many wide-eyed, innocent faces since I questioned a group of kids about the kidnapping of Mr. Adam's prize pig last Halloween. Of course the pig was returned crowned with a ribbon and hat. But this is different, isn't it? I think the best thing to do is wait a few days and question some of them again. You know whoever did this won't be able to keep quiet."

Bob was amused by the incident and murmured to himself as he returned to the café "Why didn't I think of doing that when I was in school?"

The police soon ran out of leads and placed their investigation on hold in hopes that the student or students involved would admit responsibility. Over fifty years have passed, and the mystery of, "who threw the skunk in the school house" has never been solved. Even today, there are those who swear that when the temperature and humidity are just right, you can still get a whiff of that skunk.

Hugo High School
Home of the Buffaloes

School Mascot

CHAPTER 32

Examples

Have you ever been asked to do something that you really didn't want to do? Setting a "good example" can be painful. Like the time your wife says, "You kids eat that liver. Watch your Dad." Huh!! These stories are about such situations.

My first airplane ride occurred when I was about eight years old. Arrangements for the flight were accomplished quite by accident. A gentleman who worked for my Dad was a licensed pilot. One Friday as he was leaving work, he said he was going flying the following day. He asked my brother and me if we would like to take a trip around Hugo. After much begging my Dad said it would be, "ok". It was during WW II, and the thought of going up in an airplane sparked my imagination. The plane was a two seat Piper Cub, but to me it was a P-38 flying over enemy territory. We enjoyed the trip very much, and I longed for the day I might become a pilot. Somewhere between the time of this flight and adulthood I developed a great fear of flying. I would not become a famous fighter ace after all.

Later in life my job required me to fly occasionally. I dreaded those flights. I would return from my trips totally exhausted due to the stress of flying. My wife and two boys would get a kick out of my trip report. They were always interested in hearing about my white-knuckle experiences. Some of my exaggerated tales about the people seated next to me were very funny. I witnessed first hand that fear is catching.

When the boys were eight and ten years old, I asked if they wanted to take a ride in an airplane. I wanted them to get the same thrill of flying that I had at their age. They were excited. Arrangements were made for a flight over town and the surrounding area. The pilot had a two-seat aircraft and would have to take the boys up one at a time. We were to call early the following Saturday morning. If the wind was not too strong, the flight would be on.

"Come on out; the weather is fine," was the response when we called. The boys raced to the car. As we drove away, they gave their mother a final good-bye wave.

When we arrived at the airport, the pilot greeted us, "I bet these are the boys who are going on their first airplane ride." We nodded our heads identifying ourselves as we were getting out of the car. The pilot continued, "Guess what!! I have made arrangements to fly a four-seat plane, and I will be able to take all three of you up at the same time. There will be no charge for you, Mr. Wall." I was stunned as we made our way to the plane. The boys enjoyed the flight. Upon our return home, my wife questioned the boys and they described the trip from take-off to landing. When she asked me, I said, "I felt as if I had just been served another heaping platter of liver."

We do not realize the influence we have on others. We ask ourselves what could I do or say that would affect others' behavior. Whether it is a family member or total stranger our actions are noticed. I recall going to play golf while on vacation. I didn't have a tee time and asked the pro if I could be worked in as a single. He indicated he had a threesome teeing off in a few minutes, and I could join them. He introduced us, and we teed off. We had not gone far when they opened an ice chest full of beer and offered me a Miller Lite. I thanked them, but said, "I'd rather drink water." There was drinking water located throughout the course, and I had never cared for the taste of beer. As we played, the three golfers hit some bad shots. This was followed by a string of cuss words and an occasional club-throwing. We had played several holes when I noticed they were off the side of the tee whispering. One of the men came to me and asked, "Are you a preacher?"

I told him, "No", and inquired, "Why do you ask?"

He said, "Well, we noticed you don't drink beer, and you don't swear when you hit a bad shot. Fellow, the way you play golf we felt you would be more than justified in doing both; unless you're a preacher."

When I got home, I told my wife that was the first time I'd been complimented and insulted in the same sentence. We had a big laugh.

To continue my story--before we finished the round of golf they quit cussing and throwing their clubs. Their scores began to improve. When the game was over, we shook hands, and I told them how much I appreciated them letting me join their group. Later, I realized I had influenced those guys.

Throughout my life I've faced situations like this and have been made acutely aware, "What we do and say matters."

Thankfully, I no longer have to eat liver, since the kids are grown. They never developed a taste for liver, and I still prefer water over beer. My golf game has not improved, and I've accepted the fact I'm not going to be a professional.

CHAPTER 33

Salesman of the Year

THE FRONT DOOR SLAMMED SHUT BEHIND HARVEY AS HE ENTERED the house. It was obvious that he was upset, and his mother inquired,

"What on earth is wrong? I thought the door was coming off its hinges."

"I'm going to have to start my training over. Mr. Gray says I can't work in sales again until I do. It makes me mad because I did exactly what I was taught. I even checked my notes, and sure enough, I did it right! My first summer job and this happens."

"Will you have to do the entire training over? Surely you learned some parts correctly. It doesn't seem fair to start from the beginning. Do you want me to talk to Mr. Gray?" his mother commented.

"Would you? Mr. Gray said I would have to start from day one. It's a rule at Gray's Drug. Everyone must successfully complete all the training or start over. I have stocking the shelves down pat, but that doesn't matter. Another week wasted! I guess they don't think a high school kid knows how to do anything."

"What did you do that caused the problem?" Mom questioned.

"Well, Mrs. Howard came in and wanted a bottle of her favorite perfume. I

looked in our perfume case, and we were out. According to our training we are supposed to offer a substitute if we are out of an item. We have to keep sales up."

"Did you offer a substitute?"

"Yes, I did. That is what makes me so mad! I did just what I was told to do."

"What did you offer?"

"I told her we were out of that perfume, but we had just received a shipment of milk of magnesia."

"Take the training, Son!"

CHAPTER 34

When the role is called

THERE WAS NEVER A DULL MOMENT IN THE WALL HOUSEHOLD when I was growing up. Much of our parent's time was spent running the family business. Although we were not around our parents during the day when we were young, my brother and I were always aware of the fact we were loved. There was a lot of hugging, singing, and laughter when the family was together.

We were given instructions in polite manners, right from wrong, and compassion for our fellowman. Church every Sunday was also included in our training. We were members of the Methodist Church. The congregation was small in number with an average attendance of sixty to seventy. Brother Armstrong was our preacher. In his early life he had been a real cowboy. It was not uncommon to hear stories of his time on the range sprinkled throughout his sermons. Phrases like, "Sin will stomp you down like a nine hundred pound bull at full charge" were used to illustrate a point. He was not a polished speaker, but he made the scriptures come alive, and everyone liked him. This was particularly true of the younger boys. The life of a cowboy seemed exciting.

Brother Armstrong, his wife, Bessie, and my parents were good friends. Frequently, they would have Sunday dinner with us. My brother and I raised chickens to make extra money. During the spring, fried chicken was always served when the Armstrong's were guests. Of course they had first choice from the platter of chicken. Bessie would take a breast, and Brother Armstrong's favorite was a leg and a thigh. Chicken, combined with a variety of fresh vegetables, and hot biscuits with honey made a very satisfying meal.

One Sunday the topic of Brother Armstrong's sermon was "How great it will be when we all get to heaven". He went through the congregation naming the people who will be there, "The Means family, Howard Carry, the Randolph family, the Wilson family, etc." He named everyone present except us. "Just an oversight" was the thought going through my parents' minds. He continued to preach about how wonderful heaven would be. Halfway through his sermon he threw his hands up, pointed toward the entrance to the sanctuary and said in a loud voice, "Look!! Here come the Walls, late, as usual." Of course everyone laughed, including my folks.

On the way home we talked about the sermon and the joke that had been so funny. The pastor and his wife were to have dinner with us later that day. When they arrived at our house, the meal was not ready. Dad entertained the guests in the living room while my brother and I helped mother with the table settings and food. When the call for dinner was given, the guests entered the dining room and were directed to their regular places. Portions of chicken had already been distributed to their plates. Bessie looked down and saw a chicken breast on her plate. Right in the middle of Brother Armstrong's plate, conspicuously all alone, laid the neck of the chicken! Don't tell me that revenge isn't sweet. You should have seen the satisfied smile on my mother's face.

There were no comments made about the selection of the chicken in everyone's plate. Brother Armstrong began to eat the piece that he had received. When he had consumed the last parcel of meat from the chicken neck, mother sent me to retrieve and serve a thigh and leg set aside for him in the kitchen.

Mother smiled and stated, "Those pieces must have arrived late."

CHAPTER 35

Good Advice

Tommy and Nita were engaged to be wed. They were madly in love and wanted their marriage to be successful. Nita was concerned that they might be too young and immature to undertake such a serious step. Tommy suggested they ask advice from Mr. Granger. He and his wife had the reputation of being the happiest couple in Hugo.

Tommy started the conversation, "What is your secret for a good marriage, Mr. Granger?"

He smiled and said, "Sophie and I were about your age when we got married. We had doubts about the future too. I guess most young folks do." He paused for a moment then continued, "I suppose it's different for each couple, but I can tell you what made our marriage so good. Do you think that would be helpful?"

"Oh yes! We've watched you two for years. We want the happiness you and Mrs. Granger have." Nita answered excitedly.

Pointing his finger at them, he replied, "Don't get the idea we haven't had our ups and downs. We've had our differences, but worked through them. I guess the best way to tell you our secret is to tell you a story."

Mr. Granger took a sip of coffee, cleared his throat, and began, "When we were first married, I was an avid golfer. I still am! Anyway,

Sophie said she wanted to learn how to play golf so she could be with me. I said I would teach her all I knew about the game, and we set out to play. On the first tee I gave her the usual instructions: don't move your head, keep your left arm straight, follow through, and swing easy. Well, she hit the ball, and it went about ten yards."

"'What did I do wrong?' she asked."

"You moved your head forward, I answered."

"'No I didn't,' was her emphatic reply."

"The result of her next attempt was similar to the first. 'What did I do wrong?' she questioned."

"I don't think you kept your arm straight."

"She immediately informed me, 'Yes, I did.'"

"Her third swing was much improved, but the ball only traveled twenty yards."

"'What did I do wrong that time?'"

"I think if you would swing easy and not try to kill the ball, it would do better. I said, while trying to keep my composure."

"'I did swing easy.'"

"The fourth stroke sent the ball about twenty-five yards. Once again she asked me what she had done wrong."

"Nothing, it was perfect." I stated.

"'Well, if you're not going to help me!' she declared, as she made her way to the ball."

"We finally completed nine holes, at which time she stated that she would not play anymore. She was giving up the game and going home. Of course, I went with her but was secretly overjoyed with her decision. Sophie says I expand this story every time I tell it. That's probably true, but it makes a point. Every couple should make time to be apart. Through the years Sophie has been a member of the flower club, had coffee with her friends, and read many books. She loves to read. I've had my golfing and an occasional fishing trip. Time spent apart makes the time together better. When the kids came along, that was something that bounded us more. We had to look to their future. I spent less time golfing, and Sophie had less time for her actives. It was more a family affair, but we still found some time to be alone. Yep, when I look back on our happy marriage, I think getting to play golf without Sophie was the secret."

"That's wonderful advice, and we're going to follow it. I can't tell you how much we appreciate you taking the time to talk to us. Isn't that right, Tommy?" Nita exclaimed.

Tommy agreed. As they started to leave, Mr. Granger gave Tommy a small slip of paper. Tommy read the note and handed it back to him with a smile and a hearty, "Thank you."

The note read, "Our tee time is 8:15. Don't be late."

"What did the note say, Tommy?"

"He said he thinks we're going to have a long and happy marriage!!!"

CHAPTER 36

Silver Dollar Caper

THE BEST FLOWER GARDEN, LARGEST WATERMELON, SHARPEST POCKET knife, best practical joke, best fisherman, fastest car, best cook, are a few categories that stimulate a "pride of ownership" spirit among small-town citizens. This spirit attacks young and old alike; no one is exempt. The competition goes on everyday, sometimes unnoticed, but if prominent citizens struggle for recognition, everyone follows the activity very closely.

Charlie Howard owned a service station and grocery store along the highway at the west edge of town. It was a hangout for several members of a spit-and-whittle club whose main interest was baseball. Charlie always had his radio tuned to a baseball ball game with the volume turned up so those sitting on the benches out front could hear. This provided much entertainment. Charlie loved to sit with the men when his wife was available to look after the business inside the store. Each person had their favorite team, and they enjoyed arguing the quality of their choice.

Charlie was well known for his practical jokes. He had taken a silver dollar and welded a nail to one side. He attached the dollar to the pavement between the gasoline pumps and the front door of the store. As customers approached the store, they would see the dollar and attempt to pick it up. The dollar was firmly attached, and after a few seconds they would give up. Of course the on-lookers would not make any attempt to warn the person but got a good laugh when someone realized they had been had. It was interesting to see the different reactions from the people. Some would ask if the dollar belonged to those sitting on the benches. Others would step on the dollar; look around to see if anyone was watching. Regardless of the reaction, it was always a joke that everyone took delight in observing. Most victims were good natured and took the prank in stride.

William "Bill" Smith, Frontier Bank President, stopped to buy a loaf of bread. This was unusual since his wife did their shopping at a store downtown. Bill saw the dollar, and asked if it belonged to anyone seated on the bench. Charlie thought: "To be sitting outside at this particular time, must be a gift from heaven." His main rival for the office of mayor was about to fall for his silver dollar joke.

"No, it's not mine. Does it belong to any of you guys? Charlie remarked. The remainder of those present indicated a lack of ownership. Bill smiled, and said, "This is my lucky day," and bent over to pick up the coin. After several attempts he gave up. The laughter was louder than usual. Charlie said, "You've got most every dollar in town, but that's one you won't get." Bill chuckled and went inside to make his purchase.

The very next day Bill was confronted with questions about the incident. Don's Cafe was buzzing with the story about the joke played on the bank president. It was obvious that everyone in town knew that their newly elected mayor had been bested by Charlie's prank. When questioned, Bill would laugh and say, "It was a good one all right."

The following week Charlie and his buddies were sitting outside the station when a stranger pulled up in a new Ford. When the driver got out, he looked like a giant. Six- foot- six- inches tall, broad shoulders, narrow hips. He spotted the dollar as he approached and asked, "Does this dollar belong to any of you?" Charlie and the rest of the gang indicated "No". As the man attempted to pick up the coin there was not one peep out of the onlookers. Only a thin smile greeted the man after he gave up and started toward the door. After making a purchase inside the stranger returned to his car and retrieved a hammer and large screw driver. It took only three or four hits with the hammer before the coin and nail could be pried from the payment. The stranger flipped the coin in the air, smiled, put it in his pocket and drove off.

"Why didn't you stop him Charlie?" the guys questioned.

"You've got to be kidding! Did you see the size of that man? I wouldn't have tried if he had been empty handed. I'm dang sure not going to stop him when he's holding a hammer! Why didn't you guys stop him? I noticed you didn't laugh when he couldn't pick the darn thing up. We'd already told him it didn't belong to us."

Once again, Don's Cafe was buzzing with the story of the stranger and the coin. "Hay, Charlie, I understand you are giving away silver dollars at your station. I'm going to be out there later today and expect to get one." was a common remark. It seemed the practical joke had turned on Charlie.

A couple of weeks passed and most had forgotten the silver dollar episode. It was agreed by everyone in town that the episode was a draw. Neither man had gained an advantage. Both Charlie and Bill had been victims and had taken the joke in a noble and gentlemanly manner. Conversation at Don's Cafe turned to other topics.

The subject was resurrected one week later when someone noticed a six-inch-square, framed, glass trophy case on Bill Smith's desk which contained a silver dollar with a nail welded to one side. There was an engraved notation along the base of the display which read:

Mayor's Office
Hugo, Oklahoma
"Where the streets are paved with silver"

As a famous politician once said, "To the victor go the spoils!" This Mayor agrees with that philosophy. He also has a nephew who is six-foot-six inches tall, drives a new Ford, and lives sixty-five miles from Hugo, close enough for an occasional visit and far enough to be a stranger.

CHAPTER 37

Judgment

I RECALL A VISIT I MADE TO MY HOME CHURCH SEVERAL YEARS AGO. I knew something was terribly wrong when the pastor began his sermon. I've heard sermons that pinched my toes, but this preacher left nothing unturned. His words had stripped me to the bone. I felt naked and he had just started. He covered every sin known to man, except, "You shall not kill." I got the impression he was holding his option open for that one. Mad and upset would not be adequate words to describe his condition. He said, "You can get after me all you want, but when you attack my wife, you have picked on the wrong person. I won't stand for that. Now, if you haven't been involved in slandering my wife, I apologize for this sermon." Then he reconsidered, "No, no, I don't apologize. You probably need to hear it too."

Everyone rushed out of the church after the service was over. I chased someone down, and asked what had happened to prompt such a sermon. It seems that several members had been distressed about the preacher's wife wearing shorts. She had been observed wearing shorts while working in her back-yard flower bed. After several phone calls the story had evolved to, "The preacher's wife was seen wearing shorts and a "T" shirt all over town." That was unacceptable behavior for the preacher's wife. A committee of two was formed to meet with the preacher. The discussion with the pastor and his wife was rather one-sided. The members realized their error in judgment when the true story was told. They were ashamed of their actions and asked for forgiveness. The preacher's wife said she would be willing to forgive them and hoped they had learned a lesson from the experience. The pastor said, "Not so fast! You people were more than eager to spread gossip. Now, you are going to contact every member of this church. You will explain what really happened, or rather what didn't happen. You can get the names and phone numbers from the office. When you have completed that task, ask me about forgiveness."

The two committee members were allowed to enlist others who had taken part in spreading the gossip. All the church members were contacted, and the wrong seemed to have been corrected. The sermon I had heard was to be the last mention of the incident. However, it was reported that one elderly lady contacted said, "Oh, shoot! At my age being judgmental was the only sin I had left." Hopefully, she was joking, but if I were that preacher I would save the notes on that sermon.

CHAPTER 38

Mayor's Vote

An event occurred every four years that divided the citizens of my home town into several groups. The division began when it was time to elect a new mayor. The same three men always filed for the office: Mr. Smith, Mr. Little, and Mr. Howard. They were successful business men, and each had won the office at least once. Nowhere was the division more apparent than morning coffee at Don's Café. Friends who normally had their coffee together now occupied separate tables discussing strategies for their candidate's campaign.

One year an additional candidate entered the race. Others had entered the race before, so it was not surprising that there would be four running for the office. The shock was who had filed: Benny Wills! He was considered by many to be the town jokester. He was well known for his unusual and somewhat wacky ideas. His wife Betty was a nice person. However, she was withdrawn and didn't have many friends. At times she seemed to be embarrassed by her husband's antics. Most of the town's people felt sorry for her.

There were debates, teas, rallies, and public speeches around town. Signs were displayed in front yards and on telephone poles. You would have thought they were running for President of the United States.

With the vote-getting work done, it was time to go to the poles.

Votes were counted manually and would require several hours to complete. The results would be announced the following day by John Harris, who was the chairman of the election committee.

The counting was well under way when John was informed that someone was at the door and wanted to see him. It was Benny Will's wife.

"John, I'm sorry to brother you, but I have a big problem." John could see Betty was very upset and inquired what the nature of her problem was.

"I have talked to several of my friends and have not found one who voted for my husband. I love my husband, but I'm not sure he is the best person to be mayor. I must confess, I got busy and didn't vote. Anyway, I'm afraid he will only get one vote, and everyone will know even his wife didn't vote for him. He has so much fun poked at him already; he could never live that down. It didn't occur to me that he wouldn't get some votes. Will you let me vote now?"

"There's nothing I can do, Betty. Let's hope that he did better than you think." John replied in a sympathetic tone. He returned to the vote-counting but couldn't forget the agony Betty was going through.

The next morning John was ready to announce the voting results.

"May I have your attention?" John shouted. "The results of the voting for mayor are as follows: Smith-1639, Little- 1004, Howard-482, Wills-2."

After the crowd settled, John announced, "Your new mayor is Mr. Bill Smith."

Bill came to the stage and shook hands with John. "I understood that I received 1640 votes. What happened to that other vote?" Bill whispered in a joyful tone.

"I took one vote from you and gave it to Benny," John answered.

"I don't know about that! What if that had changed the outcome? To take a vote that was rightfully mine and give it to someone else is not right!" Suddenly he appeared to be very angry.

"I know it's not right, but there were extenuating circumstances. I wouldn't have done it if it had affected the outcome. I can change the totals if you like," John confessed.

"What were the extenuating circumstances?" asked Smith.

"Let's put it this way- -would you rather the folks talk about your historic landslide victory for the next four years or the fact that Benny Wills wife didn't vote for him? That would sure make good conversation at Don's Café."

Considering the situation, Bill replied, "Case Closed! One thousand six hundred and thirty nine sounds just right."

CHAPTER 39

The Truth Revealed

THE BAPTIST CHURCH WAS FILLED TO CAPACITY. ONCE AGAIN THE small town of Hugo was mourning the loss of a long time resident. Howard Davis, the owner of the Cottonwood Club had passed away. He had been ill for just a short time, and his death was not anticipated. It seemed to most folks that it was just yesterday that he was moving about town laughing and joking with everyone.

Carol Walters was seated near the front of the church. Her mind wandered back to the last funeral she attended; her husband's. Bill Walters had been dead for two and a half years. There had been many changes in her life since but somehow, in these surroundings, it didn't seem that long ago. Seated next to her were Hank Green, and Bob and Jane Baker. These three people had helped Carol through the tough times when she needed it the most.

Carol invited Hank, Bob, and Jane to come by her house the following day for a late breakfast. She insisted that all be present and to plan for an important discussion after they had eaten. They arrived on time. Carol had been so secretive about the purpose of the meeting that they were anxious to see what she had on her mind.

After eating, Carol said, "Let's move into the living room where we can be more comfortable."

"If we don't get to the bottom of this soon, I'm going to bust! You fought off every attempt for discussion during our meal. I'm ready to talk." Hank stated.

"Well, I want you to listen rather than talk, but you can comment after I've told you what I have to say." Carol insisted.

They were seated and Carol began, "I have a confession to make. I couldn't make it until now, and you will see why in a minute. I was out there the night Bill ran off the road and was killed."

She paused to see their reaction then continued, "I had been shopping with Howard's wife. When I dropped her off outside the Cottonwood Club, I saw Bill's car and knew he was inside. I drove away as fast as possible, but he saw me leaving and caught up with me. He forced me off the road and dragged me out of the car. He proceeded to beat me."

"You don't have to do this. It's over and done with." Bob stated.

"Yes, I do and don't interrupt me until I'm through. It's not over yet. Bill had hit me and knocked me down. I had never seen him so crazy. Of course he was drunk but never like this. He kicked me. I was just about unconscious when Howard arrived from the Cottonwood Club He grabbed Bill and turned him round and told him to stop. Bill said he would get Howard next and started for him. Howard had the hickory stick he kept behind the bar and hit Bill. It seemed to daze him and brought him to his senses. Bill leaned against the car for a few minutes while Howard helped me up. Bill appeared to be all-right, and we took him to his car to sit and rest for awhile. The minute he got in the car he started it and took off. I followed and saw Bill go off the road. I went back to the Club for Howard. He told his wife to call the police while Howard and I went to the location where the car left the road. It was dark, and we couldn't see how to get down to it."

Carol was crying by now but continued. "Howard said for me to go on home because help would be there soon. We agreed that we wouldn't mention the beating incident. At that time we didn't know Bill's condition. Afterward, when we found that Bill had been killed, we thought it would be best not to say anything. I mean about the fight. I couldn't say anything until now. I think Howard saved my life that night. He's gone now, and I can get this off my mind. I have always believed that the car wreck was what killed Bill, otherwise, I couldn't have stood the silence."

Bob asked, "Are you through, because I have something to say?"

"No. Both you and Hank are lawmen, and I know you have a duty to enforce the law. I leave it up to you any action you feel is necessary. Now I'm through."

Bob was the first to speak. "I've known you were there all these years. I saw footprints in the snow that night and confirmed that they were yours the day after you and Jane got back from that shopping trip to Oklahoma City. You made the same triangle logo prints on the sidewalk when I walked you to your car. I've wanted to ask you about it many times but felt justice was done and the matter was closed. That case was not in my jurisdiction at that time, but I'm sheriff now and can speak officially. Even if you had told the whole story, no charges would have been filed. Everyone knew how Bill was, and no one would have doubted you or Howard. The worse case would have been self defense. However, I too, feel the wreck was what killed him. I think the judge's ruling of accidental death was correct. Hank, how do you feel about it?"

"I feel the same way you do. I just wish Carol didn't have this on her shoulders for the past two and a half years. You're a brave girl."

Carol said, "Jane, do you have anything to say? What you think means a great deal to me."

"I think you are wonderful for being a good, faithful friend to Howard all this time."

"I'm glad that all of you feel this way. It has been such a burden. You don't know how much I've wanted to tell someone what happened. Bob, because you were Chief of Police, at the time, I started for your office to confess but backed out. I guess I didn't trust you to keep a secret. Turns out you were all along. I should have had more faith."

"Let's talk about something else." Hank said with a grin. "For instance – Do you have any more of those home made cinnamon rolls? I think one more with a cup of coffee would get me by till lunch."

"Hank, you better watch out. You're going to ruin that thirty four inch waist. If she only has one left, I had better have it to protect you from yourself." Bob chimed in.

"We have enough for everybody to indulge. Who would like one with their coffee?" Carol inquired as she headed to the kitchen.

"I'll just have coffee." Jane answered.

Carol returned with the rolls and coffee. They sat for an hour talking about old times and changes occurring around town. It was nice for Carol to laugh and enjoy conversation again without feeling guilty.

Bob and Jane said he would have to leave but they wanted to get together again real soon. "This has been wonderful. Like old times. Carol, we're going to have to take another trip." Jane said as she got up to leave.

"Bob, can you and Jane stay for just one minute more? I have something to say to Hank, and I want you to hear it too.

"Now, Hank, you've been asking me to marry you for over a year, and I've said, "No, not now." I love you, but I couldn't marry you with this over my head. If you still want me after hearing my confession, my answer is yes. I'll understand if you say no."

"You've got to be kidding! That's all I've dreamed of for two years. I love you too! Let's go get the license now and make the announcements. I'm sure you have some plans for the wedding. We can work them out on the way!" Hank answered.

All four were thrilled, and began hugging and dancing around the room.

As Bob and Jane were leaving, Bob stated, "I feel so happy! This has been one great meeting. We got good food and solved a mystery. My two best friends are getting married. I've got to get ready to go to a wedding! Hank, who's going to be your best man? I'm available. Now, if I can just figure out who threw the skunk in the school house, my day will be perfect."

CHAPTER 40

Leaving the Nest

THERE WERE TWO WEEKS OF SCHOOL LEFT BEFORE MY HIGH SCHOOL graduation. The senior class of 1951 was looking forward to entering the real world. Some were continuing their education at college. Many of the boys were concerned with the conflict raging in Korea. I was seventeen years old, not old enough to register for the draft, but it was certainly on my mind. A navy recruiter informed my friends and me that the government would immediately freeze all service enlistments. From that point, all personnel entering the service would be assigned to the branch which had the greatest need. I had always thought that I would serve in the navy. Thinking that all recruiters surely speak truthful, two classmates and I approached our school officials with the situation. After checking our grades we were given permission to leave school two weeks early. Our grades were high enough that we would not be required to take final exams and could graduate with our class. The next hurdler would be getting permission from our parents. Much to the surprise of all, our parents agreed, reluctantly.

Having been sworn-in, we boarded a train in Dallas and headed for boot camp in San Diego. We felt fortunate to have gotten in the navy just before the big freeze. It wasn't until the train began to move that I realized my life would never be the same. I felt like a young puppy that had been locked in the back yard when suddenly the gate opened. I had a fearful feeling of the unknown, yet was anxious to experience what lay ahead. Naturally, I did not express my feelings, but suspected the others felt the same.

After two days the train arrived in San Diego about one o'clock in the morning. We were ushered to a bus bound for the Naval Training Center. By the time we were assigned sleeping quarters, it was three-thirty. At five a.m. a loud-mouthed character in a kaki uniform began banging on a metal trash can, hollering, "Rise and shine you dogs!" We were informed this person was to be our D.I. He said, "It is my job for the next sixteen weeks to make you hate me". Heck, he didn't need that much time. Three days was all it took. He was good at his job.

We were issued uniforms and necessary gear for navy living. Next stop was the barber shop. There were sixty members in our company and six barbers working. Twenty five minutes later we were all finished. I'll never forget the kid from California. He had long wavy hair and was telling the barber how to cut it. The barber listened attentively and said he knew just what he wanted. They took the art of barbering to new heights. Had they been working in a civilian shop, they would have been shot. There was not a hair over a quarter inch. The kid from California was less than that!

Over the next weeks we learned to follow orders, work as a unit, wash our clothes, make beds, and were whipped into the best physical shape we had ever been. Many of the things we were required to do didn't make sense, but we learned not to question their methods. They seem to be obsessed with the use of a square knot. Everything that was tied with rope or cord must be tied with a square knot. Another thing I didn't understand was why they made such a big deal of reveille. Our company would be dressed, had breakfast, and be marching on the parade ground when the reveille bugle sounded. It seemed to me the bugler was the only late-sleeper in camp.

During most of the time in boot camp we were restricted to the base. I was anxious to visit San Diego and see the sites. After several weeks we were given liberty. The city was nice and met my expectations. My friends and I enjoyed going into the stores looking at things that reminded us of civilian life. We noticed a small restaurant advertising food with which we were not familiar—Pizza Pie We decided to try it. The menu had words we had never seen—mozzarella, provolone, romano, parmesan, etc. There was never anything like that in Hugo. We searched the menu until we found two words we could pronounce—cheese and tomato. Each of us ordered a large cheese and tomato pizza. The waiter asked,

"Are you sure you want a large?"

We told him, "Yea. We're hungry."

When the food was delivered, we moved to separate tables in order to have room for the pizza pie. That thing must have been three feet in diameter. After we had eaten one slice, we left. We considered it a learning experience and an opportunity to provide a little entertainment for the other patrons. They seemed to be amused. We were to encounter many similar learning situations during our enlistments.

At on point we were transferred to Camp Pendleton for instruction on the rifle range. A navy man on a rifle range! What will they think of next? The first day we were taught to break down an M-1 rifle and put it back together. Some of the guys in the company had never shot a gun before and were apprehensive about qualifying. My friends and I did not worry since we were considered to be good marksman back home. However, when we saw the postage stamp size target three hundred yards down range, we became concerned. I was amazed when the target puller indicated a hit. Most everyone in the company qualified. I think that was the last time I saw an M-1 rifle during my entire enlistment.

Mail-call was one activity that brightened our spirits. A letter from love ones back home was like a breath of fresh air. We were all home sick, and news from home was just what we needed. My friends and I would share information, except the personal stuff from our girl friends. Any bit of news, regardless of significance, was welcomed and thoroughly discussed. I always felt sorry for those who never received mail. They would go off by themselves while others were reading letters. I had a new friend who was raised in Boys Town. He had no folks or girl friends. I would share some of my information about Hugo. After awhile he knew the names of many people back home. If several letters went by without the mention of someone, he would ask about them. He became very familiar with Hugo and many of the more colorful citizens of his adopted home town.

Sometime during the day we would practice marching on the

parade ground. We would do various drills honing our marching skills. Why, I don't know! We marched to music of the Naval Training Center Band. Even though the heat took a toll on us physically, I would get a chill every time they played the Star Spangled Banner. The temperature was around ninety degrees and some of the fellows would pass out if we were required to stand at attention for long periods. We were not allowed to give assistance to those who fell. They had a unit of medical personnel who would eventually attend to those in need. It seemed unkind, but it sure prevented someone from faking. No one was made seriously ill or injured due to the heat. It seemed like a waste of time, but I must admit that we became a sharp marching unit after several weeks practice.

About the time we had given up on ever getting out of boot camp, it was over. Sixteen weeks had finally passed, and it was time to go home for thirty days. One of the guys came around collecting donations to buy a gift for our DI. I asked "Walter, why give a gift to someone who has made our lives miserable?" His answer did not convince me it was the right thing to do. He collected enough to buy a nice watch. I was not one of the major contributors. When the gift was presented, the DI chewed Walter out for having the wrapping tied in a bow knot rather than a square knot. However, he overlooked the error and accepted the watch. The thought went through my mind, "Walter, you got just what you deserved."

I'm not a person to hold a grudge, but have often wondered if I met our DI today, could I resist taking a swing at him. In spite of the hardships we suffered, we had managed to survive boot camp. Afterwards, I could see that it was good for us. We had left Hugo as green kids just out of high school but had matured quickly. We were ready to take on anything that the world could throw at us.

My friends and I were separated after boot camp but managed to see each other from time to time before we finished our enlistments. When I told my Aunt Eddie I had served my time and had been discharged, she asked, "Was it an honorable discharge, son?" I laughed and assured her that it was. The navy had offered us opportunities to see much of the world. Yes, we had traveled to many wonderful locations. Some were large ultra modern cities, and others were small exotic and romantic sites. But none measured up to the ole home town.

There were costs suffered from being away from home and loved ones, but there were benefits too. My friends and I took advantage of the G.I. Bill. We finished our college education and have had successful careers in law, education, and engineering. Being in the Navy was an experience I look back on with many fond memories, and I do not regret having served. However, it would take more than a slick tongue recruiter to get me back. We're a little sharper now. We did notice new recruits coming into the training center every week for our entire sixteen weeks of boot camp. Big freeze- huh! We learned where the saying came from:

"If his lips are moving, it's a lie."

J. Wall, Arvin Rhodes, Bill McClure
Boot Camp

Bill McClure aboard ship

John Wall